19th-C

SHORT
STORIES

EDITED BY
CHRISTOPHER EDGE

OXFORD
UNIVERSITY PRESS

OXFORD
UNIVERSITY PRESS

Great Clarendon Street, Oxford, OX2 6DP,
United Kingdom

Oxford University Press is a department of the University of Oxford.
It furthers the University's objective of excellence in research, scholarship,
and education by publishing worldwide. Oxford is a registered trade mark of
Oxford University Press in the UK and in certain other countries

British Library Cataloguing in Publication Data

Data available

ISBN 978-0-19-836733-8

3 5 7 9 10 8 6 4

Printed in China by Golden Cup

Acknowledgements

We are grateful for permission to include the following copyright material in
this book:

'The Star' (first published in 1910), from The Country of the Blind and Other
Selected Stories edited by Patrick Parrinder (Penguin, 2007), reprinted by
permission of United Agents LLP on behalf of The Literary Executors of the
Estate of H G Wells.

Cover: © Andrii Muzyka / Shutterstock

Contents

Introduction

The 19th century was the golden age of the short story. From supernatural tales penned by renowned authors such as Charles Dickens to Arthur Conan Doyle's mysteries of the great detective Sherlock Holmes, the short story form flourished in the decades between 1800 and the end of Queen Victoria's reign in 1901.

At the start of the 19th century there were only a handful of magazines specializing in prose fiction where authors of short stories could find an outlet for their work. The cost of paper was high and these magazines were heavily taxed by the government, cutting publishers' profit margins. But the abolition of these taxes in the middle of the 19th century and improved methods of paper production led to an explosion of literary magazines featuring all forms of fiction. By the end of the century more than 100,000 different newspapers, magazines and periodicals had been published, giving the short story writer countless outlets for their work.

These new magazines were created to feed the growing appetite for reading amongst the general public. The Education Act of 1870 meant that all children had to attend school for a minimum of five years. This led to rising levels of literacy and a thirst for knowledge and entertainment from all sections of society. Rising wages too meant that families who previously couldn't afford to buy novels could now purchase a weekly or monthly magazine filled with serial fiction and short stories. Publications such as *The Strand* magazine, home of the Sherlock Holmes' stories, sold over half a million copies of every issue in the 1890s.

The American author Edgar Allan Poe defined the short story as a narrative which could be read in a 'single sitting' and said that most successful short stories were designed to produce a single effect in the mind of the reader. The short stories in this collection have been organized into a range of genres, each seeking to create different effects. There are ghost stories that aim to produce a frisson of horror, mysteries that seek to engage the reader's intellect, fantasy and science fiction stories to evoke a sense of wonder, and tales rooted in the reality of 19th-century life. The stories in each section have been arranged into pairs, allowing for comparisons to be drawn and enabling the reader to explore how the genre developed and changed.

In these pages you will find stories from celebrated 19th-century authors such as Charles Dickens, Mary Shelley, Wilkie Collins, Thomas Hardy, H. G. Wells, Oscar Wilde and Arthur Conan Doyle as well as some lesser known writers too. Thomas Hardy once wrote in an essay on the benefits of reading fiction:

"If we speak of deriving good from a story, we usually mean something more than the gain of pleasure during the hours of its perusal. Nevertheless, to get pleasure out of a book is a beneficial and profitable thing."

I hope the stories in this collection both give you pleasure and benefit you too.

Christopher Edge

Ghost stories

The 19th century was a period haunted by ghostly tales of death and fear. In the real world, deadly diseases stalked the streets of the rapidly growing cities, leaving the population with an unsettling understanding of the closeness of the grave. These concerns were reflected in the fiction that they read as stories of the supernatural found ever wider readerships.

At the outset of the 19th century, the ghost story's style was still rooted in Gothic tales of terror, where a romantic hero or heroine is plagued by sinister events in the Gothic setting of a castle or similarly imposing place. However, as the century wore on, the genre evolved and sensationalized settings that looked to the past for inspiration were replaced by a different style of ghost story that reflected the reality of the Victorian age.

From the mid-19th century, supernatural tales were increasingly filled with everyday details that would be familiar to the 19th-century reader. New inventions such as the railway became the setting for stories of unsettling encounters between the living and the dead, whilst dark forces lurked in familiar places such as the public house or family home.

These ghost stories appeared in the monthly magazines that became increasingly popular in the second half of the 19th century. The Christmas editions of these magazines became celebrated for their supernatural tales, with families reading these stories aloud around the fire on Christmas Eve.

As one of the most prominent writers of the Victorian age, Charles Dickens did a lot to popularize the ghost story. As the editor of magazines such as *Household Words* and *All the Year Round*, Dickens asked writers such as Wilkie Collins and Elizabeth Gaskell to contribute their own short stories in this genre, but in his own fiction Dickens also drew on supernatural elements. His most famous ghost story, *A Christmas Carol*, helped to foster the association between the festive season and tales of the supernatural, whilst in other short stories that he wrote Dickens explored the ghostly boundary between the possible and the uncanny. In his short story included in this collection, 'The Signal-man', Dickens tells the tale of a ghostly encounter on the railway that foretells a tragedy to come.

Female writers such as Elizabeth Gaskell and E. Nesbit also contributed to the development of the ghost story in the 19th century. In 'The Old Nurse's Story', first published in 1852, Gaskell revisits Gothic themes as she unfolds her tale of dark secrets and strange behaviour in the sinister Furnivall Manor. In contrast, E. Nesbit's short story, 'John Charrington's Secret', presents the happy event of a wedding, but one with an unexpected twist in the tale.

The Signal-man
by Charles Dickens

The Signal-man was first published as part of a collection in 1866. The story is likely to be partially based on a terrible train crash involving three trains in a tunnel near Brighton in 1861. Readers at the time would have been familiar with this disaster.

"Halloa! Below there!"

When he heard a voice thus calling to him, he was standing at the door of his box, with a flag in his hand, furled round its short pole. One would have thought, considering the nature of the ground, that he could not have doubted from what **quarter** the voice came; but instead of looking up to where I stood on the top of the steep cutting nearly over his head, he turned himself about, and looked down **the line**. There was something remarkable in his manner of doing so, though I could not have said for my life what. But I know it was remarkable enough to attract my notice, even though his figure was foreshortened and shadowed, down in the deep trench, and mine was high above him, so steeped in the glow of an angry sunset, that I had shaded my eyes with my hand before I saw him at all.

"Halloa! Below!"

From looking down the line, he turned himself about again, and raising his eyes, saw my figure high above him.

"Is there any path by which I can come down and speak to you?"

He looked up at me without replying, and I looked down at him without pressing him too soon with a repetition of my idle question. Just then there came a vague vibration in the earth and air, quickly changing into a violent **pulsation**, and an oncoming rush that caused me to start back, as though it had force to draw me down. When such vapour as rose to my height from this rapid train had passed me, and was skimming away over the landscape, I looked down again, and saw him refurling the flag he had shown while the train went by.

I repeated my inquiry. After a pause, during which he seemed to regard me with fixed attention, he motioned with his rolled-up flag towards a point on my level, some two or three hundred yards distant. I called down to him, "All right!" and made for that point. There, by **dint** of looking closely about me, I found a rough zigzag descending path notched out, which I followed.

The cutting was extremely deep, and unusually **precipitate**. It was made through a clammy stone, that became oozier and wetter as I went down. For these

13

reasons, I found the way long enough to give me time to recall a singular air of reluctance or compulsion with which he had pointed out the path.

When I came down low enough upon the zigzag descent to see him again, I saw that he was standing between the rails on the way by which the train had lately passed, in an attitude as if he were waiting for me to appear. He had his left hand at his chin, and that left elbow rested on his right hand, crossed over his breast. His attitude was one of such expectation and watchfulness that I stopped a moment, wondering at it.

I resumed my downward way, and stepping out upon the level of the railroad, and drawing nearer to him, saw that he was a dark sallow man, with a dark beard and rather heavy eyebrows. His post was in as solitary and dismal a place as ever I saw. On either side, a dripping-wet wall of jagged stone, excluding all view but a strip of sky; the perspective one way only a crooked **prolongation** of this great dungeon; the shorter perspective in the other direction terminating in a gloomy red light, and the gloomier entrance to a black tunnel, in whose massive architecture there was a **barbarous**, depressing, and forbidding air. So little sunlight ever found its way to this spot, that it had an earthy, deadly smell; and so much cold wind rushed through it, that it struck chill to me, as if I had left the natural world.

Before he stirred, I was near enough to him to have

touched him. Not even then removing his eyes from mine, he stepped back one step, and lifted his hand.

This was a lonesome post to occupy (I said), and it had riveted my attention when I looked down from up yonder. A visitor was a rarity, I should suppose; not an unwelcome rarity, I hoped? In me, he merely saw a man who had been shut up within narrow limits all his life, and who, being at last set free, had a newly-awakened interest in these great works. To such purpose I spoke to him; but I am far from sure of the terms I used; for, besides that I am not happy in opening any conversation, there was something in the man that daunted me.

He directed a most curious look towards the red light near the tunnel's mouth, and looked all about it, as if something were missing from it, and then looked at me.

That light was part of his charge? Was it not?

He answered in a low voice, "Don't you know it is?"

The monstrous thought came into my mind, as I **perused** the fixed eyes and the **saturnine** face, that this was a spirit, not a man. I have speculated since, whether there may have been infection in his mind.

In my turn, I stepped back. But in making the action, I detected in his eyes some latent fear of me. This put the monstrous thought to flight.

"You look at me," I said, forcing a smile, "as if you had a dread of me."

"I was doubtful," he returned, "whether I had seen you before."

"Where?"

He pointed to the red light he had looked at.

"There?" I said.

Intently watchful of me, he replied (but without sound), "Yes."

"My good fellow, what should I do there? However, be that as it may, I never was there, you may swear."

"I think I may," he rejoined. "Yes; I am sure I may."

His manner cleared, like my own. He replied to my remarks with readiness, and in well-chosen words. Had he much to do there? Yes; that was to say, he had enough responsibility to bear; but exactness and watchfulness were what was required of him, and of actual work — manual labour — he had next to none. To change that signal, to trim those lights, and to turn this iron handle now and then, was all he had to do under that head. Regarding those many long and lonely hours of which I seemed to make so much, he could only say that the routine of his life had shaped itself into that form, and he had grown used to it. He had taught himself a language down here — if only to know it by sight, and to have formed his own crude ideas of its pronunciation, could be called learning it. He had also worked at fractions and decimals, and tried a little algebra; but he was, and had been as a boy, a poor hand at figures. Was it necessary for him when on duty always to remain in that channel of damp air, and could he never rise into the sunshine from between those high stone walls? Why, that depended upon times and circumstances. Under some conditions there would be less upon the line than under others, and the same held good as to certain hours of the day and night. In bright weather, he did choose occasions for getting a little above these lower shadows; but, being at all times liable to be called by his electric bell, and at such times listening for it with redoubled anxiety, the relief was less than I would suppose.

He took me into his box, where there was a fire, a desk for an official book in which he had to make certain entries, a telegraphic instrument with its dial, face, and needles, and the little bell of which he had spoken. On my trusting that he would excuse the remark that he had been well educated, and (I hoped I might say without offence) perhaps educated above that station, he observed that instances of slight **incongruity** in such wise would rarely be found wanting among large bodies of men; that he had heard it was so in workhouses, in the police force, even in that last desperate resource, the army; and that he knew it was so, more or less, in any great railway staff. He had been, when young (if I could believe it, sitting in that hut — he scarcely could), a student of natural philosophy, and had attended lectures; but he had run wild, misused his opportunities, gone down, and never risen again. He had no complaint to offer about that. He had made his bed, and he lay upon it. It was far too late to make another.

All that I have here condensed he said in a quiet manner, with his grave dark regards divided between me and the fire. He threw in the word, "Sir," from time to time, and especially when he referred to his youth — as though to request me to understand that he claimed to be nothing but what I found him. He was several times interrupted by the little bell, and had to read off messages, and send replies. Once he had to stand without the door, and display a flag as a train passed, and make some verbal communication to the driver. In the discharge of his duties, I observed him to be remarkably exact and vigilant, breaking off his discourse at a syllable, and remaining silent until what he had to do was done.

In a word, I should have set this man down as one of the safest of men to be employed in that capacity, but for the circumstance that while he was speaking to me he twice broke off with a fallen colour, turned his face towards the little bell when it did NOT ring, opened the door of the hut (which was kept shut to exclude the unhealthy damp), and looked out towards the red light near the mouth of the tunnel. On both of those occasions, he came back to the fire with the inexplicable air upon him which I had remarked, without being able to define, when we were so far asunder.

Said I, when I rose to leave him, "You almost make me think that I have met with a contented man."

(I am afraid I must acknowledge that I said it to lead him on.)

"I believe I used to be so," he rejoined, in the low voice in which he had first spoken; "but I am troubled, sir, I am troubled."

He would have recalled the words if he could. He had said them, however, and I took them up quickly.

"With what? What is your trouble?"

"It is very difficult to impart, sir. It is very, very difficult to speak of. If ever you make me another visit, I will try to tell you."

"But I expressly intend to make you another visit. Say, when shall it be?"

"I go off early in the morning, and I shall be on again at ten tomorrow night, sir."

"I will come at eleven."

He thanked me, and went out at the door with me. "I'll show my white light, sir," he said, in his peculiar low voice, "till you have found the way up. When you have found it, don't call out! And when you are at the top, don't call out!"

His manner seemed to make the place strike colder to me, but I said no more than, "Very well."

"And when you come down tomorrow night, don't call out! Let me ask you a parting question. What made you cry, 'Halloa! Below there!' tonight?"

"Heaven knows," said I. "I cried something to that effect —"

"Not to that effect, sir. Those were the very words. I know them well."

"I admit those were the very words. I said them, no doubt, because I saw you below."

"For no other reason?"

"What other reason could I possibly have?"

"You had no feeling that they were conveyed to you in any supernatural way?"

"No."

He wished me good-night, and held up his light. I walked by the side of the down line of rails (with a very disagreeable sensation of a train coming behind me) until I found the path. It was easier to mount than to descend, and I got back to my inn without any adventure.

Punctual to my appointment, I placed my foot on the first notch of the zigzag next night, as the distant clocks were striking eleven. He was waiting for me at the bottom, with his white light on. "I have not called out," I said, when we came close together; "may I speak now?" "By all means, sir." "Good-night, then, and here's my hand." "Good-night, sir, and here's mine." With that we walked side by side to his box, entered it, closed the door, and sat down by the fire.

"I have made up my mind, sir," he began, bending forward as soon as we were seated, and speaking in a tone but a little above a whisper, "that you shall not have to ask me twice what troubles me. I took you for some one else yesterday evening. That troubles me."

"That mistake?"

"No. That someone else."

"Who is it?"

"I don't know."

"Like me?"

"I don't know. I never saw the face. The left arm is across the face, and the right arm is waved — violently waved. This way."

I followed his action with my eyes, and it was the action of an arm gesticulating, with the utmost passion and **vehemence**, "For God's sake, clear the way!"

"One moonlight night," said the man, "I was sitting here, when I heard a voice cry, 'Halloa! Below there!' I started up, looked from that door, and saw this someone else standing by the red light near the tunnel, waving as I just now showed you. The voice seemed hoarse with shouting, and it cried, 'Look out! Look out!' And then again, 'Halloa! Below there! Look out!' I caught up my lamp, turned it on red, and ran towards the figure, calling, 'What's wrong? What has happened? Where?' It stood just outside the blackness of the tunnel. I advanced so close upon it that I wondered at its keeping the sleeve across its eyes. I ran right up at it, and had my hand stretched out to pull the sleeve away, when it was gone."

"Into the tunnel?" said I.

"No. I ran on into the tunnel, five hundred yards. I stopped, and held my lamp above my head, and saw the figures of the measured distance, and saw the wet stains stealing down the walls and trickling through the arch. I ran out again faster than I had run in (for I had a mortal **abhorrence** of the place upon me), and I looked all round the red light with my own red light, and I went up the iron ladder to the gallery atop of it, and I came down again, and ran back here. I telegraphed both ways, 'An alarm has been given. Is anything wrong?' The answer came back, both ways, 'All well.'"

Resisting the slow touch of a frozen finger tracing out my spine, I showed him how that this figure must be a deception of his sense of sight; and how that figures, originating in disease of the delicate nerves that minister to the functions of the eye, were known to have often troubled patients, some of whom had become conscious of the nature of their affliction, and had even proved it by experiments upon themselves. "As to an imaginary cry," said I, "do but listen for a moment to the wind in this unnatural valley while we speak so low, and to the wild harp it makes of the telegraph wires."

That was all very well, he returned, after we had sat listening for a while, and he ought to know something of the wind and the wires — he who so often passed long winter nights there, alone and watching. But he would beg to remark that he had not finished.

I asked his pardon, and he slowly added these words, touching my arm, —

"Within six hours after the appearance, the memorable accident on this line happened, and within ten hours the dead and wounded were brought along through the tunnel over the spot where the figure had stood."

A disagreeable shudder crept over me, but I did my best against it. It was not to be denied, I rejoined, that this was a remarkable coincidence, calculated deeply to impress his mind. But it was unquestionable that remarkable coincidences did continually occur, and they must be taken into account in dealing with such a subject. Though to be sure I must admit, I added (for I thought I saw that he was going to bring the objection to bear upon me), men of common sense did not allow much for coincidences in making the ordinary calculations of life.

He again begged to remark that he had not finished.

I again begged his pardon for being betrayed into interruptions.

"This," he said, again laying his hand upon my arm, and glancing over his shoulder with hollow eyes, "was just a year ago. Six or seven months passed, and I had recovered from the surprise and shock, when one morning, as the day was breaking, I, standing at the door, looked towards the red light, and saw the spectre again." He stopped, with a fixed look at me.

"Did it cry out?"

"No. It was silent."

"Did it wave its arm?"

"No. It leaned against the shaft of the light, with both hands before the face. Like this."

Once more I followed his action with my eyes. It was an action of mourning. I have seen such an attitude in stone figures on tombs.

"Did you go up to it?"

"I came in and sat down, partly to collect my thoughts, partly because it had turned me faint. When I went to the door again, daylight was above me, and the ghost was gone."

"But nothing followed? Nothing came of this?"

He touched me on the arm with his forefinger twice or thrice giving a ghastly nod each time:-

"That very day, as a train came out of the tunnel, I noticed, at a carriage window on my side, what looked like a confusion of hands and heads, and something waved. I saw it just in time to signal the driver, Stop! He shut off, and put his brake on, but the train drifted past here a hundred and fifty yards or more. I ran after it, and, as I went along, heard terrible screams and cries. A beautiful young lady had died instantaneously in one of the compartments, and was brought in here, and laid down on this floor between us."

Involuntarily I pushed my chair back, as I looked from the boards at which he pointed to himself.

"True, sir. True. Precisely as it happened, so I tell it you."

I could think of nothing to say, to any purpose, and my mouth was very dry. The wind and the wires took up the story with a long lamenting wail.

He resumed. "Now, sir, mark this, and judge how my mind is troubled. The spectre came back a week ago. Ever since, it has been there, now and again, by fits and starts."

"At the light?"

"At the danger-light."

"What does it seem to do?"

He repeated, if possible with increased passion and vehemence, that former gesticulation of, "For God's sake, clear the way!"

Then he went on. "I have no peace or rest for it. It calls to me, for many minutes together, in an agonised manner, 'Below there! Look out! Look out!' It stands waving to me. It rings my little bell —"

I caught at that. "Did it ring your bell yesterday evening when I was here, and you went to the door?"

"Twice."

"Why, see," said I, "how your imagination misleads you. My eyes were on the bell, and my ears were open to the bell, and if I am a living man, it did *not* ring at those times. No, nor at any other time, except when it was rung in the natural course of physical things by the station communicating with you."

25

He shook his head. "I have never made a mistake as to that yet, sir. I have never confused the spectre's ring with the man's. The ghost's ring is a strange vibration in the bell that it derives from nothing else, and I have not asserted that the bell stirs to the eye. I don't wonder that you failed to hear it. But I heard it."

"And did the spectre seem to be there, when you looked out?"

"It *was* there."

"Both times?"

He repeated firmly: "Both times."

"Will you come to the door with me, and look for it now?"

He bit his under lip as though he were somewhat unwilling, but arose. I opened the door, and stood on the step, while he stood in the doorway. There was the danger-light. There was the dismal mouth of the tunnel. There were the high, wet stone walls of the cutting. There were the stars above them.

"Do you see it?" I asked him, taking particular note of his face. His eyes were prominent and strained, but not very much more so, perhaps, than my own had been when I had directed them earnestly towards the same spot.

"No," he answered. "It is not there."

"Agreed," said I.

We went in again, shut the door, and resumed our

seats. I was thinking how best to improve this advantage, if it might be called one, when he took up the conversation in such a matter-of-course way, so assuming that there could be no serious question of fact between us, that I felt myself placed in the weakest of positions.

"By this time you will fully understand, sir," he said, "that what troubles me so dreadfully is the question, What does the spectre mean?"

I was not sure, I told him, that I did fully understand.

"What is its warning against?" he said, ruminating, with his eyes on the fire, and only by times turning them on me. "What is the danger? Where is the danger? There is danger overhanging somewhere on the line. Some dreadful calamity will happen. It is not to be doubted this third time, after what has gone before. But surely this is a cruel haunting of *me*. What can I do?"

He pulled out his handkerchief, and wiped the drops from his heated forehead.

"If I telegraph danger, on either side of me, or on both, I can give no reason for it," he went on, wiping the palms of his hands. "I should get into trouble, and do no good. They would think I was mad. This is the way it would work — Message – 'Danger! Take care!' Answer – 'What Danger? Where?' Message – 'Don't know. But, for God's sake, take care!' They would displace me. What else could they do?"

His pain of mind was most pitiable to see. It was the

mental torture of a conscientious man, oppressed beyond endurance by an **unintelligible** responsibility involving life.

"When it first stood under the danger-light," he went on, putting his dark hair back from his head, and drawing his hands outward across and across his temples in an extremity of feverish distress, "why not tell me where that accident was to happen — if it must happen? Why not tell me how it could be averted — if it could have been averted? When on its second coming it hid its face, why not tell me, instead, 'She is going to die. Let them keep her at home'? If it came, on those two occasions, only to show me that its warnings were true, and so to prepare me for the third, why not warn me plainly now? And I, Lord help me! A mere poor signal-man on this solitary station! Why not go to somebody with credit to be believed, and power to act?"

When I saw him in this state, I saw that for the poor man's sake, as well as for the public safety, what I had to do for the time was to compose his mind. Therefore, setting aside all question of reality or unreality between us, I represented to him that whoever thoroughly discharged his duty must do well, and that at least it was his comfort that he understood his duty, though he did not understand these confounding appearances. In this effort I succeeded far better than in the attempt to reason him out of his conviction. He became calm; the occupations incidental to his post as the night advanced began to make larger demands on his attention: and I left him at two in the morning. I had offered to stay through the night, but he would not hear of it.

That I more than once looked back at the red light as I ascended the pathway, that I did not like the red light, and that I should have slept but poorly if my bed had been under it, I see no reason to conceal. Nor did I like the two sequences of the accident and the dead girl. I see no reason to conceal that either.

But what ran most in my thoughts was the consideration how ought I to act, having become the recipient of this disclosure? I had proved the man to be intelligent, vigilant, painstaking, and exact; but how long might he remain so, in his state of mind? Though in a subordinate position, still he held a most important trust, and would I (for instance) like to stake my own life on the chances of his continuing to execute it with precision?

Unable to overcome a feeling that there would be something treacherous in my communicating what he had told me to his superiors in the company, without first being plain with himself and proposing a middle course to him, I ultimately resolved to offer to accompany him (otherwise keeping his secret for the present) to the wisest medical practitioner we could hear of in those parts, and to take his opinion. A change in his time of duty would come round next night, he had **apprised** me, and he would be off an hour or two after sunrise, and on again soon after sunset. I had appointed to return accordingly.

Next evening was a lovely evening, and I walked out early to enjoy it. The sun was not yet quite down when I traversed the field path near the top of the deep cutting. I would extend my walk for an hour, I said to myself, half an hour on and half an hour back, and it would then be time to go to my signal-man's box.

Before pursuing my stroll, I stepped to the brink and mechanically looked down, from the point from which I had first seen him. I cannot describe the thrill that seized upon me when, close at the mouth of the tunnel, I saw the appearance of a man, with his left sleeve across his eyes, passionately waving his right arm.

The nameless horror that oppressed me passed in a moment, for in a moment I saw that this appearance of a man was a man indeed, and that there was a little group of other men, standing at a short distance, to whom he seemed to be rehearsing the gesture he made. The danger-light was not yet lighted. Against its shaft, a little low hut, entirely new to me, had been made of some wooden supports and tarpaulin. It looked no bigger than a bed.

With an irresistible sense that something was wrong, with a flashing **self-reproachful** fear that fatal mischief had come of my leaving the man there, and causing no one to be sent to overlook or correct what he did. I descended the notched path with all the speed I could make.

"What is the matter?" I asked the men.

"Signalman killed this morning, sir."

"Not the man belonging to that box?"

"Yes, sir."

"Not the man I know?"

"You will recognise him, sir, if you knew him," said the man who spoke for the others, solemnly uncovering his own head and raising an end of the tarpaulin, "for his face is quite composed."

"'Oh', how did this happen, how did this happen?" I asked, turning from one to another as the hut closed in again.

"He was cut down by an engine, sir. No man in England knew his work better. But somehow he was not clear of the outer rail. It was just at broad day. He had struck the light, and had the lamp in his hand. As the engine came out of the tunnel, his back was towards her, and she cut him down. That man drove her, and was showing how it happened. Show the gentleman, Tom."

The man, who wore rough dark dress, stepped back to his former place at the mouth of the tunnel.

"Coming round the curve in the tunnel, sir," he said, "I saw him at the end, like as if I saw him down a perspective-glass. There was no time to check speed, and I knew him to be very careful. As he didn't seem to take heed of the whistle, I shut it off when we were running down upon him, and called to him as loud as I could call."

"What did you say?"

"I said, 'Below there! Look out! Look out! For God's sake, clear the way!'"

I started.

"Ah! it was a dreadful time, sir. I never left off calling to him. I put this arm before my eyes not to see, and I waved this arm to the last; but it was no use."

Without prolonging the narrative to dwell on any one of its curious circumstances more than on any other, I may, in closing it, point out the coincidence that the warning of the engine-driver included, not only the words which the unfortunate signalman had repeated to me as haunting him, but also the words which I myself — not he — had attached, and that only in my own mind, to the gesticulation he had imitated.

---

quarter direction
the line the railway line or track
pulsation throbbing
dint by means of
precipitate steep
prolongation extension
barbarous uncivilized, harsh
perused examined carefully
saturnine gloomy
incongruity something out of place, that doesn't fit in its location or situation
vehemence forcefulness
abhorrence hatred
unintelligible impossible to understand
apprised informed
self-reproachful blaming oneself

John Charrington's Wedding
by Edith Nesbit

> *John Charrington's Wedding* was first published in *Temple Bar* magazine in 1891. In the 19th century some people held a prejudice against reading fiction as it wasn't seen as an activity that would improve your intellect, so many short stories were presented as if they were based on true events, as is the case in this story.

No one ever thought that May Forster would marry John Charrington; but he thought differently, and things which John Charrington intended had a **queer** way of coming to pass. He asked her to marry him before he went up to Oxford. She laughed and refused him. He asked her again next time he came home. Again she laughed, tossed her dainty blonde head and again refused. A third time he asked her; she said it was becoming a confirmed bad habit, and laughed at him more than ever.

John was not the only man who wanted to marry her: she was the belle of our village coterie, and we were all in love with her more or less; it was a sort of fashion, like **masher collars** or **Inverness capes**. Therefore we were as much annoyed as surprised when John Charrington walked into our little local Club — we held it in a loft over the saddler's, I remember — and invited us all to his wedding.

'Your wedding?'

'You don't mean it?'

'Who's the happy fair? When's it to be?'

John Charrington filled his pipe and lighted it before he replied. Then he said —

'I'm sorry to deprive you fellows of your only joke — but Miss Forster and I are to be married in September.'

'You don't mean it?'

'He's **got the mitten** again, and it's turned his head.'

'No,' I said, rising, 'I see it's true. Lend me a pistol, someone — or a first-class fare to the other end of Nowhere. Charrington has bewitched the only pretty girl in our twenty-mile radius. Was it **mesmerism**, or a love-potion, Jack?'

'Neither, sir, but a gift you'll never have—perseverance — and the best luck a man ever had in this world.'

There was something in his voice that silenced me, and all **chaff** of the other fellows failed to draw him further.

The queer thing about it was that when we congratulated Miss Forster, she blushed and smiled and dimpled, for all the world as though she were in love with him, and had been in love with him all the time. Upon my word, I think she had. Women are strange creatures.

We were all asked to the wedding. In Brixham everyone who was anybody knew everybody else who was anyone. My sisters were, I truly believe, more interested in the *trousseau* than the bride herself, and I was to be best man. The coming marriage was much canvassed at afternoon tea-tables, and at our little Club over the saddler's, and the question was always asked, 'Does she care for him?'

I used to ask that question myself in the early days of their engagement, but after a certain evening in August I never asked it again. I was coming home from the Club through the churchyard. Our church is on a thyme-grown hill, and the turf about it is so thick and soft that one's footsteps are noiseless.

I made no sound as I vaulted the low lichened wall, and threaded my way between the tombstones. It was at the same instant that I heard John Charrington's voice, and saw her face. May was sitting on a low flat gravestone with the full splendour of the western sun upon her *mignonne* face. Its expression ended, at once and for ever, any question of love for him; it was transfigured to a beauty I should not have believed possible, even to that beautiful little face.

John lay at her feet, and it was his voice that broke the stillness of the golden August evening.

'My dear, my dear, I believe I should come back from the dead if you wanted me!'

I coughed at once to indicate my presence, and passed on into the shadow fully enlightened.

The wedding was to be early in September. Two days before I had to run up to town on business. The train was late, of course, for we are on the South-Eastern, and as I stood grumbling with my watch in my hand, whom should I see but John Charrington and May Forster. They were walking up and down the unfrequented end of the platform, arm in arm, looking into each other's eyes, careless of the sympathetic interest of the porters.

Of course I knew better than to hesitate a moment before burying myself in the booking-office, and it was not till the train drew up at the platform, that I obtrusively passed the pair with my Gladstone, and took the corner in a first-class smoking-carriage. I did this with as good an air of not seeing them as I could assume. I pride myself on my discretion, but if John were travelling alone I wanted his company. I had it.

'Hullo, old man,' came his cheery voice as he swung his bag into my carriage; 'here's luck; I was expecting a dull journey!'

'Where are you off to?' I asked, discretion still bidding me turn my eyes away, though I saw, without looking, that hers were red-rimmed.

'To old Branbridge's,' he answered, shutting the door and leaning out for a last word with his sweetheart.

'Oh, I wish you wouldn't go, John,' she was saying in a low, earnest voice. 'I feel certain something will happen.'

'Do you think I should let anything happen to keep me, and the day after tomorrow our wedding-day?'

'Don't go,' she answered, with a pleading intensity which would have sent my Gladstone onto the platform and me after it. But she wasn't speaking to me. John Charrington was made differently: he rarely changed his opinions, never his resolutions.

He only stroked the little ungloved hands that lay on the carriage door.

'I must, May. The old boy's been awfully good to me, and now he's dying I must go and see him, but I shall come home in time for —' the rest of the parting was lost in a whisper and in the rattling lurch of the starting train.

'You're sure to come?' she spoke as the train moved.

'Nothing shall keep me,' he answered; and we steamed out. After he had seen the last of the little figure on the platform he leaned back in his corner and kept silence for a minute.

When he spoke it was to explain to me that his godfather, whose heir he was, lay dying at Peasmarsh Place, some fifty miles away, and had sent for John, and John had felt bound to go.

'I shall be surely back tomorrow,' he said, 'or, if not, the day after, in heaps of time. Thank Heaven, one hasn't to get up in the middle of the night to get married nowadays!'

'And suppose Mr Branbridge dies?'

'Alive or dead I mean to be married on Thursday!' John answered, lighting a cigar and unfolding *The Times*.

At Peasmarsh station we said 'goodbye', and he got out, and I saw him ride off; I went on to London, where I stayed the night.

When I got home the next afternoon, a very wet one, by the way, my sister greeted me with —

'Where's Charrington?'

'Goodness knows,' I answered testily. Every man, since **Cain**, has resented that kind of question.

'I thought you might have heard from him,' she went on, 'as you're to give him away tomorrow.'

'Isn't he back?' I asked, for I had confidently expected to find him at home.

'No, Geoffrey,' — my sister Fanny always had a way of jumping to conclusions, especially such conclusions as were least favourable to her fellow-creatures — 'he has not returned, and, what is more, you may depend upon it he won't. You mark my words, there'll be no wedding tomorrow.'

My sister Fanny has a power of annoying me which no other human being possesses.

'You mark my words,' I retorted with asperity, 'you had better give up making such a thundering idiot of yourself. There'll be more wedding tomorrow than ever you'll take the first part in.' A prophecy which, by the way, came true.

But though I could snarl confidently to my sister, I did not feel so comfortable when, late that night, I, standing on the doorstep of John's house, heard that he had not returned. I went home gloomily through the rain. Next morning brought a brilliant blue sky, gold sun, and all such softness of air and beauty of cloud as go to make up a perfect day. I woke with a vague feeling of having gone to bed anxious, and of being rather averse to facing that anxiety in the light of full wakefulness.

But with my shaving-water came a note from John which relieved my mind and sent me up to the Forsters with a light heart.

May was in the garden. I saw her blue gown through the hollyhocks as the lodge gates swung to behind me. So I did not go up to the house, but turned aside down the turfed path.

'He's written to you too,' she said, without preliminary greeting, when I reached her side.

'Yes, I'm to meet him at the station at three, and come straight on to the church.'

Her face looked pale, but there was a brightness in her eyes, and a tender quiver about the mouth that spoke of renewed happiness.

'Mr Branbridge begged him so to stay another night that he had not the heart to refuse,' she went on. 'He is so kind, but I wish he hadn't stayed.'

I was at the station at half-past two. I felt rather

annoyed with John. It seemed a sort of slight to the beautiful girl who loved him, that he should come as it were out of breath, and with the dust of travel upon him to take her hand, which some of us would have given the best years of our lives to take.

But when the three o'clock train glided in, and glided out again having brought no passengers to our little station, I was more than annoyed. There was no other train for thirty-five minutes; I calculated that, with much hurry, we might just get to the church in time for the ceremony; but, oh, what a fool to miss that first train! What other man could have done it?

That thirty-five minutes seemed a year, as I wandered round the station reading the advertisements and the time-tables, and the company's bye-laws, and getting more and more angry with John Charrington. This confidence in his own power of getting everything he wanted the minute he wanted it was leading him too far. I hate waiting. Everyone does, but I believe I hate it more than anyone else. The three thirty-five was late, of course.

I ground my pipe between my teeth and stamped with impatience as I watched the signals. Click. The signal went down. Five minutes later I flung myself into the carriage that I had brought for John.

'Drive to the church!' I said, as someone shut the door. 'Mr Charrington hasn't come by this train.'

Anxiety now replaced anger. What had become of the man? Could he have been taken suddenly ill? I had never known him have a day's illness in his life. And even so he might have telegraphed. Some awful accident must have happened to him. The thought that he had played her false never — no, not for a moment, entered my head. Yes, something terrible had happened to him, and on me lay the task of telling his bride. I tell you, I almost wished the carriage would upset and break my head so that someone else might tell her, not I, who — but that's nothing to do with the story.

It was five minutes to four as we drew up at the churchyard gate. A double row of eager onlookers lined the path from **lych-gate** to porch. I sprang from the carriage and passed up between them. Our gardener had a good front place near the door. I stopped.

'Are they waiting still, Byles?' I asked, simply to gain time, for of course I knew they were by the waiting crowd's attentive attitude.

'Waiting, sir? No, no, sir; why, it must be over by now.'

'Over! Then Mr Charrington's come?'

'To the minute, sir; must have missed you somehow, and, I say, sir,' lowering his voice, 'I never see Mr John the least bit so afore, but my opinion is he's been drinking pretty free. His clothes was all dusty and his face like a sheet. I tell you I didn't like the looks of him at all, and the folks inside are saying all sorts of things. You'll see, something's gone very wrong with Mr John, and he's tried liquor. He looked like a ghost, and in he went with his eyes straight before him, with never a look or a word for none of us; him that was always such a gentleman!'

I had never heard Byles make so long a speech. The crowd in the churchyard were talking in whispers and getting ready rice and slippers to throw at the bride and bridegroom. The ringers were ready with their hands on the ropes to ring out the merry peal as the bride and bridegroom should come out.

A murmur from the church announced them; out they came, Byles was right. John Charrington did not look himself. There was dust on his coat, his hair was disarranged. He seemed to have been in some row, for there was a black mark above his eyebrow. He was deathly pale. But his pallor was not greater than that of the bride, who might have been carved in ivory — dress, veil, orange blossoms and all.

As they passed out the ringers stooped — there were six of them — and then, on the ears expecting the **gay** wedding peal, came the slow tolling of the passing bell.

A thrill of horror at so foolish a jest from the ringers passed through us all. But the ringers themselves dropped the ropes and fled like rabbits down the belfry stairs.

The bride shuddered, and grey shadows came about her mouth, but the bridegroom led her on down the path where the people stood with the handfuls of rice; but the handfuls were never thrown, and the wedding-bells never rang. In vain the ringers were urged to remedy their mistake: they protested with many whispered expletives that they would see themselves further first.

In a hush like the hush in the chamber of death the bridal pair passed into their carriage and its door slammed behind them.

Then the tongues were loosed. A **babel** of anger, wonder, conjecture from the guests and the spectators.

'If I'd seen his condition, sir,' said old Forster to me as we drove off, 'I would have stretched him on the floor of the church, sir, by Heaven I would, before I'd have let him marry my daughter!'

Then he put his head out of the window.

'Drive like hell,' he cried to the coachman; 'don't spare the horses.'

He was obeyed. We passed the bride's carriage. I forbore to look at it, and old Forster turned his head away and swore. We reached home before it.

We stood in the doorway, in the blazing afternoon sun, and in about half a minute we heard wheels crunching the gravel. When the carriage stopped in front of the steps old Forster and I ran down.

'Great Heaven, the carriage is empty! And yet —'

43

I had the door open in a minute, and this is what I saw —

No sign of John Charrington; and of May, his wife only a huddled heap of white satin lying half on the floor of the carriage and half on the seat.

'I drove straight here, sir,' said the coachman, as the bride's father lifted her out; 'and I'll swear no one got out of the carriage.'

We carried her into the house in her bridal dress and drew back her veil. I saw her face. Shall I ever forget it? white, white and drawn with agony and horror, bearing such a look of terror as I have never seen since except in dreams. And her hair, her radiant blonde hair, I tell you it was white like snow.

As we stood, her father and I, half mad with the horror and mystery of it, a boy came up the avenue — a telegraph boy. They brought the orange envelope to me. I tore it open.

'Mr Charrington was thrown from his horse on his way to the station at half-past one. Killed on the spot!'

And he was married to May Forster in our parish church at half-past three, in presence of half the parish.

'I shall be married, dead, or alive!'

What had passed in that carriage on the homeward drive? No one knows — no one will ever know. Oh, May! oh, my dear!

Before a week was over they laid her beside her

husband in our little churchyard on the thyme-covered hill — the churchyard where they had kept their love-**trysts**.

Thus was accomplished John Charrington's wedding.

queer strange
masher collar a style of very high collar
Inverness cape a style of waterproof coat
got the mitten been jilted or rejected
mesmerism hypnotism
chaff mockery
trousseau a bride's outfit including the wedding dress
Cain biblical character who killed his brother Abel
lych-gate gateway at the entrance to a church
gay happy
babel noise made by a number of voices
trysts meetings

Mystery stories

As the streets of 19th-century Britain witnessed a rising tide of criminality leading to the establishment of full-time police forces, so 19th-century readers turned to stories of crime and mystery in the fiction that they read. In the first half of the century, 'penny dreadfuls' or 'penny bloods' containing stories of highwaymen, pirates and notorious criminals became extremely popular amongst working-class readers. Costing just a penny for a single weekly issue, these eight-page booklets with black-and-white illustrations were often blamed for leading young readers into a life of crime, lured by the lurid tales of lawlessness found within their pages.

However it was in the form of the novel that the mystery genre began to take shape in the middle of the 19th century. Charles Dickens introduced the character of a detective, Inspector Bucket, in his novel *Bleak House* (first published in 1853), with the honest and tenacious policeman solving the murder that is the mystery at the heart of story. Dickens's fellow author and friend Wilkie Collins established several more conventions of the genre in his 1868 novel *The Moonstone*, the thrilling tale of the search for a priceless stolen diamond and the thief behind the crime.

With his creation of the legendary detective, Sherlock Holmes, Arthur Conan Doyle was the author who brought the mystery genre to even greater heights of success. First introduced in two novels, *A Study in Scarlet* and *The Sign of the Four*, Sherlock Holmes featured in a dozen short stories published by Doyle in the pages of *The Strand* magazine between July 1891 and June 1892. With his great intellect and keen deductive mind, Sherlock Holmes' adventures entranced the reading public and each issue of *The Strand* magazine at this time sold more than half a million copies.

In the short story included in this collection, 'The Adventure of the Speckled Band', Holmes investigates a case brought to him by a frightened young woman, Helen Stoner, whose sister has died in mysterious circumstances.

The success of the Sherlock Holmes stories spawned countless imitators in the pages of rival literary magazines. From the female detective, Lady Molly of Scotland Yard, to Raffles, the gentleman thief, many authors tried to replicate Doyle's bestselling formula, but few of their stories achieved the same hold on the public's imagination.

The second story in this section, 'A Terribly Strange Bed' by Wilkie Collins, predates Sherlock Holmes' first appearance by 35 years, but this sinister tale of crime and mystery shares a key similarity with 'The Adventure of the Speckled Band' ...

The Adventure of the Speckled Band
by Arthur Conan Doyle

The Adventure of the Speckled Band first appeared in *The Strand* magazine in February 1892. With its ingenious plot and dastardly villain, this story quickly became one of Arthur Conan Doyle's most celebrated mysteries and was actually chosen by the author himself as one of his favourite Sherlock Holmes stories.

In glancing over my notes of the seventy odd cases in which I have during the last eight years studied the methods of my friend Sherlock Holmes, I find many tragic, some comic, a large number merely strange, but none commonplace; for, working as he did rather for the love of his art than for the acquirement of wealth, he refused to associate himself with any investigation which did not tend towards the unusual, and even the fantastic. Of all these varied cases, however, I cannot recall any which presented more singular features than that which was associated with the well-known Surrey family of the Roylotts of Stoke Moran. The events in question occurred in the early days of my association with Holmes, when we were sharing rooms as bachelors, in Baker Street. It is possible that I might have placed them upon record before, but a promise of secrecy was made at the time, from which I have only been freed during the last month by the untimely death of the lady to whom the pledge was given. It is perhaps as well that the facts should now come to light, for I have reasons to know there are widespread rumours as to the death of Dr Grimesby Roylott which tend to make the matter even more terrible than the truth.

It was early in April in the year '83 that I woke one morning to find Sherlock Holmes standing, fully dressed, by the side of my bed. He was a late riser as a rule, and, as the clock on the mantelpiece showed me that it was only a quarter past seven, I blinked up at him in some surprise, and perhaps just a little resentment, for I was myself regular in my habits.

"Very sorry to knock you up, Watson," said he, "but it's the common lot this morning. Mrs Hudson has been knocked up, she retorted upon me, and I on you."

"What is it, then? A fire?"

"No, a client. It seems that a young lady has arrived in a considerable state of excitement, who insists upon seeing me. She is waiting now in the sitting-room. Now, when young ladies wander about the metropolis at this hour of the morning, and knock sleepy people up out of their beds, I presume that it is something very pressing which they have to communicate. Should it prove to be an interesting case, you would, I am sure, wish to follow it from the outset. I thought, at any rate, that I should call you and give you the chance."

"My dear fellow, I would not miss it for anything."

I had no keener pleasure than in following Holmes in his professional investigations, and in admiring the rapid deductions, as swift as intuitions, and yet always founded on a logical basis, with which he unravelled the problems which were submitted to him. I rapidly threw on my clothes, and was ready in a few minutes to accompany my friend down to the sitting-room. A lady dressed in black and heavily veiled, who had been sitting in the window, rose as we entered.

"Good morning, madam," said Holmes cheerily. "My name is Sherlock Holmes. This is my intimate friend and associate, Dr Watson, before whom you can speak as freely as before myself. Ha, I am glad to see that Mrs Hudson has had the good sense to light the fire. Pray draw up to it, and I shall order you a cup of hot coffee, for I observe that you are shivering."

"It is not cold which makes me shiver," said the woman in a low voice, changing her seat as requested.

"What then?"

"It is fear, Mr Holmes. It is terror." She raised her veil as she spoke, and we could see that she was indeed in a pitiable state of agitation, her face all drawn and grey, with restless, frightened eyes, like those of some hunted animal. Her features and figure were those of a woman of thirty, but her hair was shot with premature grey, and her expression was weary and haggard. Sherlock Holmes ran her over with one of his quick, all-comprehensive glances.

"You must not fear," said he, soothingly, bending forward and patting her forearm. "We shall soon set matters right, I have no doubt. You have come in by train this morning, I see."

"You know me, then?"

"No, but I observe the second half of a return ticket in the palm of your left glove. You must have started early, and yet you had a good drive in a dog-cart, along heavy roads, before you reached the station."

The lady gave a violent **start** and stared in bewilderment at my companion.

"There is no mystery, my dear madam," said he, smiling. "The left arm of your jacket is spattered with mud in no less than seven places. The marks are perfectly fresh. There is no vehicle save a dog-cart which throws up mud in that way, and then only when you sit on the left-hand side of the driver."

"Whatever your reasons may be, you are perfectly correct," said she. "I started from home before six, reached Leatherhead at twenty past, and came in by the first train to Waterloo. Sir, I can stand this strain no longer, I shall go mad if it continues. I have no one to turn to—none, save only one, who cares for me, and he, poor fellow, can be of little aid. I have heard of you, Mr Holmes; I have heard of you from Mrs Farintosh, whom you helped in the hour of her sore need. It was from her that I had your address. Oh, sir, do you not think that you could help me too, and at least throw a little light through the dense darkness which surrounds me? At present it is out of my power to reward you for your services, but in a month or two weeks I shall be married, with the control of my own income, and then at least you shall not find me ungrateful."

Holmes turned to his desk, and unlocking it, drew out a small case-book, which he consulted.

"Farintosh," said he. "Ah, yes, I recall the case; it was concerned with an opal tiara. I think it was before your time, Watson. I can only say, madam, that I shall be happy to devote the same care to your case as I did to that of your friend. As to reward, my profession is its own reward; but you are at liberty to **defray** whatever expenses I may be put to, at the time which suits you best. And now I beg that you will lay before us everything that may help us in forming an opinion upon the matter."

"Alas!" replied our visitor. "The very horror of my situation lies in the fact that my fears are so vague, and my suspicions depend so entirely upon small points, which might seem trivial to another, that even he to whom of all others I have a right to look for help and advice looks upon all that I tell him about it as the fancies of a nervous woman. He does not say so, but I can read it from his soothing answers and averted eyes. But I have heard, Mr Holmes, that you can see deeply into the **manifold** wickedness of the human heart. You may advise me how to walk amid the dangers which encompass me."

"I am all attention, madam."

"My name is Helen Stoner, and I am living with my step-father, who is the last survivor of one of the oldest Saxon families in England; the Roylotts of Stoke Moran, on the western border of Surrey."

Holmes nodded his head. "The name is familiar to me," said he.

"The family was at one time among the richest in England, and the estate extended over the borders into Berkshire in the north, and Hampshire in the west. In the last century, however, four successive heirs were of a **dissolute** and wasteful disposition, and the family ruin was eventually completed by a gambler in the days of the Regency. Nothing was left save a few acres of ground, and the two-hundred-year-old house, which is itself crushed under a heavy mortgage. The last squire dragged out his existence there, living the horrible life of an aristocratic pauper; but his only son, my step-father, seeing that he must adapt himself to the new conditions, obtained an advance from a relative, which enabled him to take a medical degree and went out to Calcutta, where, by his professional skill and his force of character, he established a large practice. In a fit of anger, however, caused by some robberies which had been perpetrated in the house, he beat his native butler to death, and narrowly escaped a capital sentence. As it was, he suffered a long term of imprisonment, and afterwards returned to England a morose and disappointed man.

"When Dr Roylott was in India he married my mother, Mrs Stoner, the young widow of Major-General Stoner, of the Bengal Artillery. My sister Julia and I were twins, and we were only two years old at the time of my mother's re-marriage. She had a considerable sum of money, not less than a thousand pounds a year, and this she bequeathed to Dr Roylott entirely while we resided with him, with a provision that a certain annual sum should be allowed to each of us in the event of our marriage. Shortly after our return to England my mother died—she was killed eight years ago in a railway accident near Crewe. Dr Roylott then abandoned his attempts to establish himself in practice in London, and took us to live with him in the ancestral house at Stoke Moran. The money which my mother had left was enough for all our wants, and there seemed to be no obstacle to our happiness.

"But a terrible change came over our stepfather about this time. Instead of making friends and exchanging visits with our neighbours, who had at first been overjoyed to see a Roylott of Stoke Moran back in the old family seat, he shut himself up in his house, and seldom came out save to indulge in ferocious quarrels with whoever might cross his path. Violence of temper approaching to mania has been hereditary in the men of the family, and in my stepfather's case it had, I believe, been intensified by his long residence in the tropics. A series of disgraceful brawls took place, two of which ended in the police-court, until at last he became the terror of the village, and the folks would fly at his approach, for he is a man of immense strength, and absolutely uncontrollable in his anger.

"Last week he hurled the local blacksmith over a parapet into a stream and it was only by paying over all the money which I could gather together that I was able to avert another public exposure. He had no friends at all save the wandering gipsies, and he would give these vagabonds leave to encamp upon the few acres of bramble-covered land which represent the family estate, and would accept in return the hospitality of their tents, wandering away with them sometimes for weeks on end. He has a passion also for Indian animals, which are sent over to him by a correspondent, and he has at this moment a cheetah and a baboon, which wander freely over his grounds and are feared by the villagers almost as much as their master.

"You can imagine from what I say that my poor sister Julia and I had no great pleasure in our lives. No servant would stay with us, and for a long time we did all the work of the house. She was but thirty at the time of her death, and yet her hair had already begun to whiten, even as mine has."

"Your sister is dead, then?"

"She died just two years ago, and it is of her death that I wish to speak to you. You can understand that, living the life which I have described, we were little likely to see anyone of our own age and position. We had, however, an aunt, my mother's maiden sister, Miss Honoria Westphail, who lives near Harrow, and we were occasionally allowed to pay short visits at this lady's house. Julia went there at Christmas two years ago, and met there a half-pay Major of Marines, to whom she became engaged. My stepfather learned of the engagement when my sister returned, and offered no objection to the marriage; but within a fortnight of the day which had been fixed for the wedding, the terrible event occurred which has deprived me of my only companion."

Sherlock Holmes had been leaning back in his chair with his eyes closed, and his head sunk in a cushion, but he half opened his lids now and glanced across at his visitor.

"Pray be precise as to details," said he.

"It is easy for me to be so, for every event of that dreadful time is seared into my memory. The manor house is, as I have already said, very old, and only one wing is now inhabited. The bedrooms in this wing are on the ground floor, the sitting-rooms being in the central block of the buildings. Of these bedrooms the first is Dr Roylott's, the second my sister's, and the third my own. There is no communication between them, but they all open out into the same corridor. Do I make myself plain?"

"Perfectly so."

"The windows of the three rooms open out upon the lawn. That fatal night Dr Roylott had gone to his room early, though we knew that he had not retired to rest, for my sister was troubled by the smell of the strong Indian cigars which it was his custom to smoke. She left her room, therefore, and came into mine, where she sat for some time, chatting about her approaching wedding. At eleven o'clock she rose to leave me, but she paused at the door and looked back.

"'Tell me, Helen,' said she, 'have you ever heard anyone whistle in the dead of the night?'

"'Never,' said I.

"'I suppose that you could not possibly whistle yourself in your sleep?'

"'Certainly not. But why?'

"'Because during the last few nights I have always, about three in the morning, heard a low clear whistle. I am a light sleeper, and it has awakened me. I cannot tell where it came from—perhaps from the next room, perhaps from the lawn. I thought that I would just ask you whether you had heard it.'

"'No, I have not. It must be those wretched gipsies in the plantation.'

"'Very likely. And yet if it were on the lawn I wonder that you did not hear it also.'

"'Ah, but I sleep more heavily than you.'

"'Well, it is of no great consequence, at any rate,' she smiled back at me, closed my door, and a few moments later I heard her key turn in the lock."

"Indeed," said Holmes. "Was it your custom always to lock yourselves in at night?"

"Always."

"And why?"

"I think that I mentioned to you that the Doctor kept a cheetah and a baboon. We had no feeling of security unless our doors were locked."

"Quite so. Pray proceed with your statement."

"I could not sleep that night. A vague feeling of impending misfortune impressed me. My sister and I, you will recollect, were twins, and you know how subtle are the links which bind two souls which are so closely allied. It was a wild night. The wind was howling outside, and the rain was beating and splashing against the windows. Suddenly, amidst all the hubbub of the gale, there burst forth the wild scream of a terrified woman. I knew that it was my sister's voice. I sprang from my bed, wrapped a shawl round me, and rushed into the corridor. As I opened my door I seemed to hear a low whistle, such as my sister described, and a few moments later a clanging sound, as if a mass of metal had fallen. As I ran down the passage my sister's door was unlocked, and revolved slowly upon its hinges. I stared at it horror-stricken, not knowing what was about to issue from it. By the light of the corridor lamp I saw my sister appear at the opening, her face blanched with terror, her hands groping for help, her whole figure swaying to and fro like that of a drunkard. I ran to her and threw my arms round her, but at that moment her knees seemed to give way and she fell to the ground. She writhed as one who is in terrible pain, and her limbs were dreadfully convulsed. At first I thought that she had not recognized me, but as I bent over her she suddenly shrieked out in a voice which I shall never forget, 'Oh, my God! Helen! It was the band! The speckled band!' There was something else which she would fain have said, and she stabbed with her finger into the air in the direction of the Doctor's room, but a fresh convulsion seized her and choked her words. I rushed out, calling loudly for my stepfather, and I met him hastening from his room in his dressing-gown. When he reached my sister's side she was unconscious, and though he poured brandy down her throat, and sent for medical aid from the village, all efforts were in vain, for she slowly sank and died without having recovered her consciousness. Such was the dreadful end of my beloved sister."

"One moment," said Holmes: "are you sure about this whistle and metallic sound? Could you swear to it?"

"That was what the county coroner asked me at the inquiry. It is my strong impression that I heard it, and yet among the crash of the gale, and the creaking of an old house, I may possibly have been deceived."

"Was your sister dressed?"

"No, she was in her nightdress. In her right hand was found the charred stump of a match, and in her left a matchbox."

"Showing that she had struck a light and looked about her when the alarm took place. That is important. And what conclusions did the coroner come to?"

"He investigated the case with great care, for Dr Roylott's conduct had long been notorious in the county, but he was unable to find any satisfactory cause of death. My evidence showed that the door had been fastened upon the inner side, and the windows were blocked by old-fashioned shutters with broad iron bars, which were secured every night. The walls were carefully sounded, and were shown to be quite solid all round, and the flooring was also thoroughly examined, with the same result. The chimney is wide, but is barred up by four large staples. It is certain, therefore, that my sister was quite alone when she met her end. Besides, there were no marks of any violence upon her."

"How about poison?"

"The doctors examined her for it, but without success."

"What do you think that this unfortunate lady died of, then?"

"It is my belief that she died of pure fear and nervous shock, though what it was which frightened her I cannot imagine."

"Were there gipsies in the plantation at the time?"

"Yes, there are nearly always some there."

"Ah, and what did you gather from this allusion to a band—a speckled band?"

"Sometimes I have thought that it was merely the wild talk of delirium, sometimes that it may have referred to some band of people, perhaps to these very gipsies in the plantation. I do not know whether the spotted handkerchiefs which so many of them wear over their heads might have suggested the strange adjective which she used."

Holmes shook his head like a man who is far from being satisfied.

"These are very deep waters," said he; "pray go on with your narrative."

"Two years have passed since then, and my life has been until lately lonelier than ever. A month ago, however, a dear friend, whom I have known for many years, has done me the honor to ask my hand in marriage. His name is Armitage—Percy Armitage—the second son of Mr Armitage, of Crane Water, near Reading. My stepfather has offered no opposition to the match, and we are to be married in the course of the spring. Two days ago some repairs were started in the west wing of the building, and my bedroom wall has been pierced, so that I have had to move into the chamber in which my sister died, and to sleep in the very bed in which she slept. Imagine, then, my thrill of terror when last night, as I lay awake, thinking over her terrible fate, I suddenly heard in the silence of the night the low whistle which had been the herald of her own death. I sprang up and lit the lamp, but nothing was to be seen in the room. I was too shaken to go to bed again, however, so I dressed, and as soon as it was daylight I slipped down, got a dog-cart at the Crown Inn, which is opposite, and drove to Leatherhead, from whence I have come on this morning, with the one object of seeing you and asking your advice."

"You have done wisely," said my friend. "But have you told me all?"

"Yes, all."

"Miss Roylott, you have not. You are **screening** your stepfather."

"Why, what do you mean?"

For answer Holmes pushed back the frill of black lace which fringed the hand that lay upon our visitor's knee. Five little livid spots, the marks of four fingers and a thumb, were printed upon the white wrist.

"You have been cruelly used," said Holmes.

The lady colored deeply, and covered over her injured wrist. "He is a hard man," she said, "and perhaps he hardly knows his own strength."

There was a long silence, during which Holmes leaned his chin upon his hands and stared into the crackling fire.

"This is a very deep business," he said at last. "There are a thousand details which I should desire to know before I decide upon our course of action. Yet we have not a moment to lose. If we were to come to Stoke Moran to-day, would it be possible for us to see over these rooms without the knowledge of your stepfather?"

"As it happens, he spoke of coming into town to-day upon some most important business. It is probable that he will be away all day, and that there would be nothing to disturb you. We have a housekeeper now, but she is old and foolish, and I could easily get her out of the way."

"Excellent. You are not averse to this trip, Watson?"

"By no means."

"Then we shall both come. What are you going to do yourself?"

"I have one or two things which I would wish to do now that I am in town. But I shall return by the twelve o'clock train, so as to be there in time for your coming."

"And you may expect us early in the afternoon. I have myself some small business matters to attend to. Will you not wait and breakfast?"

"No, I must go. My heart is lightened already since I

have confided my trouble to you. I shall look forward to seeing you again this afternoon." She dropped her thick black veil over her face, and glided from the room.

"And what do you think of it all, Watson?" asked Sherlock Holmes, leaning back in his chair.

"It seems to me to be a most dark and sinister business."

"Dark enough, and sinister enough."

"Yet if the lady is correct in saying that the flooring and walls are sound, and that the door, window, and chimney are impassable, then her sister must have been undoubtedly alone when she met her mysterious end."

"What becomes, then, of these nocturnal whistles, and what of the very peculiar words of the dying woman?"

"I cannot think."

"When you combine the ideas of whistles at night, the presence of a band of gipsies who are on intimate terms with this old doctor, the fact that we have every reason to believe that the doctor has an interest in preventing his stepdaughter's marriage, the dying allusion to a band, and finally, the fact that Miss Helen Stoner heard a metallic clang, which might have been caused by one of those metal bars which secured the shutters falling back into their place, I think that there is good ground to think that the mystery may be cleared along those lines."

"But what, then, did the gipsies do?"

"I cannot imagine."

"I see many objections to any such a theory."

"And so do I. It is precisely for that reason that we are going to Stoke Moran this day. I want to see whether the objections are fatal, or if they may be explained away. But what in the name of the devil!"

The **ejaculation** had been drawn from my companion by the fact that our door had been suddenly dashed open, and that a huge man had framed himself in the aperture. His costume was a peculiar mixture of the professional and of the agricultural, having a black top-hat, a long frock-coat, and a pair of high gaiters, with a hunting-crop swinging in his hand. So tall was he that his hat actually brushed the cross bar of the doorway, and his breadth seemed to span it across from side to side. A large face, seared with a thousand wrinkles, burned yellow with the sun, and marked with every evil passion, was turned from one to the other of us, while his deep-set, bile-shot eyes, and his high thin fleshless nose, gave him somewhat the resemblance to a fierce old bird of prey.

"Which of you is Holmes?" asked this apparition.

"My name, sir, but you have the advantage of me," said my companion, quietly.

"I am Dr Grimesby Roylott, of Stoke Moran."

"Indeed, Doctor," said Holmes blandly. "Pray take a seat."

"I will do nothing of the kind. My stepdaughter has been here. I have traced her. What has she been saying to you?"

"It is a little cold for the time of the year," said Holmes.

"What has she been saying to you?" screamed the old man furiously.

"But I have heard that the crocuses promise well," continued my companion imperturbably.

"Ha! You put me off, do you?" said our new visitor, taking a step forward, and shaking his hunting-crop. "I know you, you scoundrel! I have heard of you before. You are Holmes the meddler."

My friend smiled.

"Holmes the busybody!"

His smile broadened.

"Holmes the Scotland Yard jack-in-office!"

Holmes chuckled heartily. "Your conversation is most entertaining," said he. "When you go out close the door, for there is a decided draught."

"I will go when I have said my say. Don't you dare to meddle with my affairs. I know that Miss Stoner has been here—I traced her! I am a dangerous man to fall foul of! See here." He stepped swiftly forward, seized the poker, and bent it into a curve with his huge brown hands.

"See that you keep yourself out of my grip," he snarled, and hurling the twisted poker into the fireplace, he strode out of the room.

"He seems a very amiable person," said Holmes, laughing. "I am not quite so bulky, but if he had remained I might have shown him that my grip was not much more feeble than his own." As he spoke he picked up the steel poker, and with a sudden effort straightened it out again.

"Fancy his having the insolence to confound me with the official detective force! This incident gives zest to our investigation, however, and I only trust that our little friend will not suffer from her imprudence in allowing this brute to trace her. And now, Watson, we shall order breakfast, and afterwards I shall walk down to Doctors' Commons, where I hope to get some data which may help us in this matter."

It was nearly one o'clock when Sherlock Holmes returned from his excursion. He held in his hand a sheet of blue paper, scrawled over with notes and figures.

"I have seen the will of the deceased wife," said he. "To determine its exact meaning I have been obliged to work out the present prices of the investments with which it is concerned. The total income, which at the time of the wife's death was little short of 1100 pounds, is now through the fall in agricultural prices not more than 750 pounds. Each daughter can claim an income of 250 pounds, in case of marriage. It is evident, therefore, that if both girls had married, this beauty would have had a mere pittance, while even one of them would cripple him to a very serious extent. My morning's work has not been wasted, since it has proved that he has the very strongest motives for standing in the way of anything of the sort.

And now, Watson, this is too serious for dawdling, especially as the old man is aware that we are interesting ourselves in his affairs, so if you are ready we shall call a cab and drive to Waterloo. I should be very much obliged if you would slip your revolver into your pocket. An **Eley's No. 2** is an excellent argument with gentlemen who can twist steel pokers into knots. That and a tooth-brush are, I think, all that we need."

At Waterloo we were fortunate in catching a train for Leatherhead, where we hired a trap at the station inn, and drove for four or five miles through the lovely Surrey lanes. It was a perfect day, with a bright sun and a few fleecy clouds in the heavens. The trees and wayside hedges were just throwing out their first green shoots, and the air was full of the pleasant smell of the moist earth. To me at least there was a strange contrast between the sweet promise of the spring and this sinister quest upon which we were engaged. My companion sat in the front of the trap, his arms folded, his hat pulled down over his eyes, and his chin sunk upon his breast, buried in the deepest thought. Suddenly, however, he started, tapped me on the shoulder, and pointed over the meadows

"Look there!" said he.

A heavily timbered park stretched up in a gentle slope, thickening into a grove at the highest point. From amidst the branches there jutted out the grey gables and high roof-tree of a very old mansion.

"Stoke Moran?" said he.

"Yes, sir, that be the house of Dr Grimesby Roylott," remarked the driver.

"There is some building going on there," said Holmes: "that is where we are going."

"There's the village," said the driver, pointing to a cluster of roofs some distance to the left; "but if you want to get to the house, you'll find it shorter to get over this stile, and so by the foot-path over the fields. There it is, where the lady is walking."

"And the lady, I fancy, is Miss Stoner," observed Holmes, shading his eyes. "Yes, I think we had better do as you suggest."

We got off, paid our fare, and the **trap** rattled back on its way to Leatherhead.

"I thought it as well," said Holmes, as we climbed the stile, "that this fellow should think we had come here as architects, or on some definite business. It may stop his gossip. Good-afternoon, Miss Stoner. You see that we have been as good as our word."

Our client of the morning had hurried forward to meet us with a face which spoke her joy. "I have been waiting so eagerly for you," she cried, shaking hands with us warmly. "All has turned out splendidly. Dr Roylott has gone to town, and it is unlikely that he will be back before evening."

"We have had the pleasure of making the Doctor's

acquaintance," said Holmes, and in a few words he sketched out what had occurred. Miss Stoner turned white to the lips as she listened.

"Good heavens!" she cried, "he has followed me, then."

"So it appears."

"He is so cunning that I never know when I am safe from him. What will he say when he returns?"

"He must guard himself, for he may find that there is someone more cunning than himself upon his track. You must lock yourself up from him to-night. If he is violent, we shall take you away to your aunt's at Harrow. Now, we must make the best use of our time, so kindly take us at once to the rooms which we are to examine."

The building was of grey, lichen-blotched stone, with a high central portion, and two curving wings, like the claws of a crab, thrown out on each side. In one of these wings the windows were broken, and blocked with wooden boards, while the roof was partly caved in, a picture of ruin. The central portion was in little better repair, but the right-hand block was comparatively modern, and the blinds in the windows, with the blue smoke curling up from the chimneys, showed that this was where the family resided. Some scaffolding had been erected against the end wall, and the stone-work had been broken into, but there were no signs of any workmen at the moment of our visit. Holmes walked slowly up and down the ill-trimmed lawn and examined with deep attention the outsides of the windows.

"This, I take it, belongs to the room in which you used to sleep, the centre one to your sister's, and the one next to the main building to Dr Roylott's chamber?"

"Exactly so. But I am now sleeping in the middle one."

"Pending the alterations, as I understand. By the way, there does not seem to be any very pressing need for repairs at that end wall."

"There were none. I believe that it was an excuse to move me from my room."

"Ah! that is suggestive. Now, on the other side of this narrow wing runs the corridor from which these three rooms open. There are windows in it, of course?"

"Yes, but very small ones. Too narrow for anyone to pass through."

"As you both locked your doors at night, your rooms were unapproachable from that side. Now, would you have the kindness to go into your room and bar your shutters."

Miss Stoner did so, and Holmes, after a careful examination through the open window, endeavoured in every way to force the shutter open, but without success. There was no slit through which a knife could be passed to raise the bar. Then with his lens he tested the hinges, but they were of solid iron, built firmly into the massive masonry. "Hum!" said he, scratching his chin in some perplexity, "my theory certainly presents some difficulties. No one could pass these shutters if they were bolted. Well, we shall see if the inside throws any light upon the matter."

A small side-door led into the whitewashed corridor from which the three bedrooms opened. Holmes refused to examine the third chamber, so we passed at once to the second, that in which Miss Stoner was now sleeping, and in which her sister had met with her fate. It was a homely little room, with a low ceiling and a gaping fireplace, after the fashion of old country houses. A brown chest of drawers stood in one corner, a narrow white-counterpaned bed in another, and a dressing-table on the left-hand side of the window. These articles, with two small wickerwork chairs, made up all the furniture in the room save for a square of Wilton carpet in the centre. The boards round and the panelling of the walls were brown, worm-eaten oak, so old and discoloured that it may have dated from the original building of the house. Holmes drew one of the chairs into a corner and sat silent, while his eyes travelled round and round and up and down, taking in every detail of the apartment.

"Where does that bell communicate with?" he asked at last, pointing to a thick bell-rope which hung down beside the bed, the tassel actually lying upon the pillow.

"It goes to the housekeeper's room."

"It looks newer than the other things?"

"Yes, it was only put there a couple of years ago."

"Your sister asked for it, I suppose?"

"No, I never heard of her using it. We used always to get what we wanted for ourselves."

"Indeed, it seemed unnecessary to put so nice a bell-pull there. You will excuse me for a few minutes while I satisfy myself as to this floor." He threw himself down upon his face with his lens in his hand and crawled swiftly backwards and forwards, examining minutely the cracks between the boards. Then he did the same with the woodwork with which the chamber was panelled. Finally he walked over to the bed and spent some time in staring at it and in running his eye up and down the wall. Finally he took the bell-rope in his hand and gave it a brisk tug.

"Why, it's a dummy," said he.

"Won't it ring?"

"No, it is not even attached to a wire. This is very interesting. You can see now that it is fastened to a hook just above where the little opening of the ventilator is."

"How very absurd! I never noticed that before."

"Very strange!" muttered Holmes, pulling at the rope. "There are one or two very singular points about this room. For example, what a fool a builder must be to open a ventilator into another room, when, with the same trouble, he might have communicated with the outside air!"

"That is also quite modern," said the lady.

"Done about the same time as the bell-rope?" remarked Holmes.

"Yes, there were several little changes carried out about that time."

"They seem to have been of a most interesting character—dummy bell-ropes, and ventilators which do not ventilate. With your permission, Miss Stoner, we shall now carry our researches into the inner apartment."

Dr Grimesby Roylott's chamber was larger than that of his step-daughter, but was as plainly furnished. A camp bed, a small wooden shelf full of books, mostly of a technical character, an armchair beside the bed, a plain wooden chair against the wall, a round table, and a large iron safe were the principal things which met the eye. Holmes walked slowly round and examined each and all of them with the keenest interest.

"What's in here?" he asked, tapping the safe.

"My stepfather's business papers."

"Oh! you have seen inside then?"

"Only once, some years ago. I remember that it was full of papers."

"There isn't a cat in it, for example?"

"No. What a strange idea!"

"Well, look at this!" He took up a small saucer of milk which stood on the top of it.

"No; we don't keep a cat. But there is a cheetah and a baboon."

"Ah, yes, of course! Well, a cheetah is just a big cat, and yet a saucer of milk does not go very far in satisfying its wants, I daresay. There is one point which I should wish to determine." He squatted down in front of the wooden chair, and examined the seat of it with the greatest attention.

"Thank you. That is quite settled," said he, rising and putting his lens in his pocket. "Hello! here is something interesting!"

The object which had caught his eye was a small dog lash hung on one corner of the bed. The lash, however, was curled upon itself, and tied so as to make a loop of whipcord.

"What do you make of that, Watson?"

"It's a common enough lash. But I don't know why if should be tied."

"That is not quite so common, is it? Ah, me! it's a wicked world, and when a clever man turns his brains to crime it is the worst of all. I think that I have seen enough now, Miss Stoner, and with your permission, we shall walk out upon the lawn."

I had never seen my friend's face so grim, or his brow so dark, as it was when we turned from the scene of his investigation. We had walked several times up and down the lawn, neither Miss Stoner nor myself liking to break in upon his thoughts before he roused himself from his reverie.

"It is very essential, Miss Stoner," said he, "that you should absolutely follow my advice in every respect."

"I shall most certainly do so."

"The matter is too serious for any hesitation. Your life may depend upon your compliance."

"I assure you that I am in your hands."

"In the first place, both my friend and I must spend the night in your room."

Both Miss Stoner and I gazed at him in astonishment.

"Yes, it must be so. Let me explain. I believe that that is the village inn over there?"

"Yes, that is the Crown."

"Very good. Your windows would be visible from there?"

"Certainly."

"You must confine yourself to your room, on pretence of a headache, when your stepfather comes back. Then when you hear him **retire** for the night, you must open the shutters of your window, undo the hasp, put your lamp there as a signal to us, and then withdraw quietly with everything which you are likely to want into the room which you used to occupy. I have no doubt that, in spite of the repairs, you could manage there for one night."

"Oh, yes, easily."

"The rest you will leave in our hands."

"But what will you do?"

"We shall spend the night in your room, and we shall investigate the cause of this noise which has disturbed you."

"I believe, Mr Holmes, that you have already made up your mind," said Miss Stoner, laying her hand upon my companion's sleeve.

"Perhaps I have."

"Then for pity's sake tell me what was the cause of my sister's death."

"I should prefer to have clearer proofs before I speak."

"You can at least tell me whether my own thought is correct, and if she died from some sudden fright."

"No, I do not think so. I think that there was probably some more tangible cause. And now, Miss Stoner, we must leave you for if Dr Roylott returned and saw us, our journey would be in vain. Good-bye, and be brave, for if you will do what I have told you, you may rest assured that we shall soon drive away the dangers that threaten you."

Sherlock Holmes and I had no difficulty in engaging a bedroom and sitting-room at the Crown Inn. They were on the upper floor, and from our window we could command a view of the avenue gate, and of the inhabited wing of Stoke Moran Manor House. At dusk we saw Dr

Grimesby Roylott drive past, his huge form looming up beside the little figure of the lad who drove him. The boy had some slight difficulty in undoing the heavy iron gates, and we heard the hoarse roar of the Doctor's voice and saw the fury with which he shook his clinched fists at him. The trap drove on, and a few minutes later we saw a sudden light spring up among the trees as the lamp was lit in one of the sitting-rooms.

"Do you know, Watson," said Holmes, as we sat together in the gathering darkness, "I have really some scruples as to taking you tonight. There is a distinct element of danger."

"Can I be of assistance?"

"Your presence might be invaluable."

"Then I shall certainly come."

"It is very kind of you."

"You speak of danger. You have evidently seen more in these rooms than was visible to me."

"No, but I fancy that I may have deduced a little more. I imagine that you saw all that I did."

"I saw nothing remarkable save the bell-rope, and what purpose that could answer I confess is more than I can imagine."

"You saw the ventilator, too?"

"Yes, but I do not think that it is such a very unusual thing to have a small opening between two rooms. It was so small that a rat could hardly pass through."

"I knew that we should find a ventilator before ever we came to Stoke Moran."

"My dear Holmes!"

"Oh, yes, I did. You remember in her statement she said that her sister could smell Dr Roylott's cigar. Now, of course that suggests at once that there must be a communication between the two rooms. It could only be a small one, or it would have been remarked upon at the Coroner's inquiry. I deduced a ventilator."

"But what harm can there be in that?"

"Well, there is at least a curious coincidence of dates. A ventilator is made, a cord is hung, and a lady who sleeps in the bed dies. Does not that strike you?"

"I cannot as yet see any connection."

"Did you observe anything very peculiar about that bed?"

"No."

"It was clamped to the floor. Did you ever see a bed fastened like that before?"

"I cannot say that I have."

"The lady could not move her bed. It must always be in the same relative position to the ventilator and to the rope—or so we may call it, since it was clearly never meant for a bell-pull."

"Holmes," I cried, "I seem to see dimly what you are hitting at. We are only just in time to prevent some subtle and horrible crime."

"Subtle enough, and horrible enough. When a doctor does go wrong, he is the first of criminals. He has nerve and he has knowledge. Palmer and Pritchard were among the heads of their profession. This man strikes even deeper, but, I think, Watson, that we shall be able to strike deeper still. But we shall have horrors enough before the night is over: for goodness' sake let us have a quiet pipe, and turn our minds for a few hours to something more cheerful."

About nine o'clock the light among the trees was extinguished, and all was dark in the direction of the Manor House. Two hours passed slowly away, and then, suddenly, just at the stroke of eleven, a single bright light shone out right in front of us.

"That is our signal," said Holmes, springing to his feet; "it comes from the middle window."

As we passed out he exchanged a few words with the landlord, explaining that we were going on a late visit to an acquaintance, and that it was possible that we might spend the night there. A moment later we were out on the dark road, a chill wind blowing in our faces, and one yellow light twinkling in front of us through the gloom to guide us on our sombre errand.

There was little difficulty in entering the grounds, for unrepaired breaches gaped in the old park wall. Making our way among the trees, we reached the lawn, crossed it, and were about to enter through the window when out from a clump of laurel bushes there darted what seemed to be a hideous and distorted child, who threw itself upon the grass with writhing limbs, and then ran swiftly across the lawn into the darkness.

"My God!" I whispered, "did you see it?"

Holmes was for the moment as startled as I. His hand closed like a vice upon my wrist in his agitation. Then he broke into a low laugh, and put his lips to my ear.

"It is a nice household," he murmured. "That is the baboon."

I had forgotten the strange pets which the doctor affected. There was a cheetah, too; perhaps we might find it upon our shoulders at any moment. I confess that I felt easier in my mind when, after following Holmes's example and slipping off my shoes, I found myself inside the bedroom. My companion noiselessly closed the shutters, moved the lamp on to the table, and cast his eyes round the room. All was as we had seen it in the day-time. Then creeping up to me and making a trumpet of his hand, he whispered into my ear again so gently that it was all that I could do to distinguish the words:

"The least sound would be fatal to our plans."

I nodded to show that I had heard.

"We must sit without a light. He would see it through the ventilator."

I nodded again.

"Do not go asleep; your very life may depend upon it. Have your pistol ready in case we should need it. I will sit on the side of the bed, and you in that chair."

I took out my revolver and laid it on the corner of the table.

Holmes had brought up a long thin cane, and this he placed upon the bed beside him. By it he laid the box of matches and the stump of a candle. Then he turned down the lamp and we were left in darkness.

How shall I ever forget that dreadful vigil? I could not hear a sound, not even the drawing of a breath, and yet I knew that my companion sat open-eyed, within a few feet of me, in the same state of nervous tension in which I was myself. The shutters cut off the least ray of light, and we waited in absolute darkness.

From outside came the occasional cry of a night-bird, and once at our very window a long, drawn cat-like whine, which told us that the cheetah was indeed at liberty. Far away we could hear the deep tones of the parish clock, which boomed out every quarter of an hour. How long they seemed, those quarters! Twelve struck, and one, and two, and three, and still we sat waiting silently for whatever might befall.

Suddenly there was the momentary gleam of a light up in the direction of the ventilator, which vanished immediately, but was succeeded by a strong smell of burning oil and heated metal. Someone in the next room had lit a dark lantern. I heard a gentle sound of movement, and then all was silent once more, though the smell grew stronger. For half an hour I sat with straining ears. Then suddenly another sound became audible—a very gentle, soothing sound, like that of a small jet of steam escaping continually from a kettle. The instant that we heard it, Holmes sprang from the bed, struck a match, and lashed furiously with his cane at the bell-pull.

"You see it, Watson?" he yelled. "You see it?"

But I saw nothing. At the moment when Holmes struck the light I heard a low, clear whistle, but the sudden glare flashing into my weary eyes made it impossible for me to tell what it was at which my friend lashed so savagely. I could, however, see that his face was deadly pale, and filled with horror and loathing.

He had ceased to strike, and was gazing up at the ventilator, when suddenly there broke from the silence of the night the most horrible cry to which I have ever listened. It swelled up louder and louder, a hoarse yell of pain and fear and anger all mingled in the one dreadful shriek. They say that away down in the village, and even in the distant parsonage, that cry raised the sleepers from their beds. It struck cold to our hearts, and I stood gazing at Holmes, and he at me, until the last echoes of it had died away into the silence from which it rose.

"What can it mean?" I gasped.

"It means that it is all over," Holmes answered. "And

perhaps, after all, it is for the best. Take your pistol, and we will enter Dr Roylott's room."

With a grave face he lit the lamp, and led the way down the corridor. Twice he struck at the chamber door without any reply from within. Then he turned the handle and entered, I at his heels, with the cocked pistol in my hand.

It was a **singular** sight which met our eyes. On the table stood a dark lantern with the shutter half open, throwing a brilliant beam of light upon the iron safe, the door of which was ajar. Beside this table, on the wooden chair, sat Dr Grimesby Roylott clad in a long grey dressing-gown, his bare ankles protruding beneath, and his feet thrust into red heelless Turkish slippers. Across his lap lay the short stock with the long lash which we had noticed during the day. His chin was cocked upwards and his eyes were fixed in a dreadful rigid stare at the corner of the ceiling. Round his brow he had a peculiar yellow band, with brownish speckles, which seemed to be bound tightly round his head. As we entered he made neither sound nor motion.

"The band! the speckled band!" whispered Holmes.

I took a step forward: in an instant his strange headgear began to move, and there reared itself from among his hair the squat diamond-shaped head and puffed neck of a loathsome serpent.

"It is a swamp adder!" cried Holmes— "the deadliest

snake in India. He has died within ten seconds of being bitten. Violence does, in truth, recoil upon the violent, and the schemer falls into the pit which he digs for another. Let us thrust this creature back into its den, and we can then remove Miss Stoner to some place of shelter and let the county police know what has happened."

As he spoke he drew the dog-whip swiftly from the dead man's lap, and throwing the noose round the reptile's neck, he drew it from its horrid perch, and carrying it at arm's length, threw it into the iron safe, which he closed upon it.

Such are the true facts of the death of Dr Grimesby Roylott, of Stoke Moran. It is not necessary that I should prolong a narrative which has already run to too great a length by telling how we broke the sad news to the terrified girl, how we conveyed her by the morning train to the care of her good aunt at Harrow, of how the slow process of official inquiry came to the conclusion that the doctor met his fate while indiscreetly playing with a dangerous pet. The little which I had yet to learn of the case was told me by Sherlock Holmes as we travelled back next day.

"I had," said he, "come to an entirely erroneous conclusion which shows, my dear Watson, how dangerous it always is to reason from insufficient data. The presence of the gipsies, and the use of the word 'band,' which was used by the poor girl, no doubt to explain the appearance which she had caught a horrid glimpse of by the light of her match, were sufficient to put me upon an entirely wrong scent. I can only claim the merit that I instantly reconsidered my position when, however, it became clear to me that whatever danger threatened an occupant of the room could not come either from the window or the door. My attention was speedily drawn, as I have already remarked to you, to this ventilator, and to the bell-rope which hung down to the bed. The discovery that this was a dummy, and that the bed was clamped to the floor, instantly gave rise to the suspicion that the rope was there as a bridge for something passing through the hole and coming to the bed. The idea of a snake instantly occurred to me, and when I coupled it with my knowledge that the Doctor was furnished with a supply of creatures from India, I felt that I was probably on the right track. The idea of using a form of poison which could not possibly be discovered by any chemical test was just such a one as would occur to a clever and ruthless man who had had an Eastern training. The rapidity with which such a poison would take effect would also, from his point of view, be an advantage. It would be a sharp-eyed coroner, indeed who could distinguish the two little dark punctures which would show where the poison fangs had done their work. Then I thought of the whistle. Of course, he must recall the snake before the morning light revealed it to the victim. He had trained it, probably by the use of the milk which we saw, to return to him when summoned. He would put it through this ventilator at the hour that he thought best, with the certainty that it would crawl down the rope, and land on the bed. It might or might not bite the occupant, perhaps she might escape every night for a week, but sooner or later she must fall a victim.

"I had come to these conclusions before ever I had entered his room. An inspection of his chair showed me that he had been in the habit of standing on it, which, of course, would be necessary in order that he should reach the ventilator. The sight of the safe, the saucer of milk, and the loop of whipcord were really enough to finally dispel any doubts which may have remained. The metallic clang heard by Miss Stoner was obviously caused by her stepfather hastily closing the door of his safe upon its terrible occupant. Having once made up my mind, you know the steps which I took in order to put the matter to the proof. I heard the creature hiss, as I have no doubt that you did also, and I instantly lit the light and attacked it."

"With the result of driving it through the ventilator."

"And also with the result of causing it to turn upon its master at the other side. Some of the blows of my cane came home, and roused its snakish temper, so that it flew upon the first person it saw. In this way I am no doubt indirectly responsible for Dr Grimesby Roylott's death, and I cannot say that it is likely to weigh very heavily upon my conscience."

start a sudden movement
defray provide money to pay expenses
manifold many and various
dissolute immoral
screening protecting
ejaculation something said suddenly
Eley's No. 2 a type of revolver also known as a Webley's No. 2
trap a two-wheeled carriage pulled by a horse
retire to go to bed
singular extraordinary

A Terribly Strange Bed
by Wilkie Collins

A Terribly Strange Bed first appeared in the April 1852 edition of *Household Words*, a magazine edited by Wilkie Collins' friend and fellow author, Charles Dickens. The story is set in Paris and narrated by a young man who is staying in the city and presents the events of the tale as fact, a technique commonly used in short stories at this time.

Shortly after my education at college was finished, I happened to be staying at Paris with an English friend. We were both young men then, and lived, I am afraid, rather a wild life, in the delightful city of our sojourn. One night we were idling about the neighbourhood of the Palais Royal, doubtful to what amusement we should next betake ourselves. My friend proposed a visit to Frascati's; but his suggestion was not to my taste. I knew Frascati's, as the French saying is, by heart; had lost and won plenty of **five-franc pieces** there, merely for amusement's sake, until it was amusement no longer, and was thoroughly tired, in fact, of all the ghastly respectabilities of such a social anomaly as a respectable gambling-house. "For Heaven's sake," said I to my friend, "let us go somewhere

where we can see a little genuine, blackguard, poverty-stricken gaming with no false gingerbread glitter thrown over it all. Let us get away from fashionable Frascati's, to a house where they don't mind letting in a man with a ragged coat, or a man with no coat, ragged or otherwise."

"Very well," said my friend, "we needn't go out of the Palais Royal to find the sort of company you want. Here's the place just before us; as **blackguard** a place, by all report, as you could possibly wish to see." In another minute we arrived at the door and entered the house, the back of which you have drawn in your sketch.

When we got upstairs, and had left our hats and sticks with the doorkeeper, we were admitted into the chief gambling-room. We did not find many people assembled there. But, few as the men were who looked up at us on our entrance, they were all types—lamentably true types—of their respective classes.

We had come to see blackguards; but these men were something worse. There is a comic side, more or less appreciable, in all blackguardism—here there was nothing but tragedy—mute, weird tragedy. The quiet in the room was horrible. The thin, haggard, long-haired young man, whose sunken eyes fiercely watched the turning up of the cards, never spoke; the flabby, fat-faced, pimply player, who pricked his piece of **pasteboard** perseveringly, to register how often black won, and how often red—never spoke; the dirty, wrinkled old man, with the vulture eyes and the darned great-coat, who had lost his last *sou*, and still looked on desperately, after he could play no longer—never spoke. Even the voice of the croupier sounded as if it were strangely dulled and thickened in the atmosphere of the room. I had entered the place to laugh, but the spectacle before me was something to weep over. I soon found it necessary to take refuge in excitement from the depression of spirits which was fast stealing on me. Unfortunately I sought the nearest excitement, by going to the table and beginning to play. Still more unfortunately, as the event will show, I won—won prodigiously; won incredibly; won at such a rate that the regular players at the table crowded round me; and staring at my stakes with hungry, superstitious eyes, whispered to one another that the English stranger was going to break the bank.

The game was *Rouge et Noir*. I had played at it in every city in Europe, without, however, the care or the wish to study the Theory of Chances—that philosopher's stone of all gamblers! And a gambler, in the strict sense of the word, I had never been. I was heart-whole from the corroding passion for play. My gaming was a mere idle amusement. I never resorted to it by necessity, because I never knew what it was to want money. I never practiced it so incessantly as to lose more than I could afford, or to gain more than I could coolly pocket without being thrown off my balance by my good luck. In short,

I had **hitherto** frequented gambling-tables—just as I frequented ball-rooms and opera-houses—because they amused me, and because I had nothing better to do with my leisure hours.

But on this occasion it was very different—now, for the first time in my life, I felt what the passion for play really was. My success first bewildered, and then, in the most literal meaning of the word, intoxicated me. Incredible as it may appear, it is nevertheless true, that I only lost when I attempted to estimate chances, and played according to previous calculation. If I left everything to luck, and staked without any care or consideration, I was sure to win—to win in the face of every recognized probability in favour of the bank. At first some of the men present ventured their money safely enough on my colour; but I speedily increased my stakes to sums which they dared not risk. One after another they left off playing, and breathlessly looked on at my game.

Still, time after time, I staked higher and higher, and still won. The excitement in the room rose to fever pitch. The silence was interrupted by a deep-muttered chorus of oaths and exclamations in different languages, every time the gold was shovelled across to my side of the table—even the **imperturbable** croupier dashed his rake on the floor in a (French) fury of astonishment at my success. But one man present preserved his self-possession, and that man was my friend. He came to my side, and whispering in English, begged me to leave the place, satisfied with what I had already gained. I must do him the justice to say that he repeated his warnings and **entreaties** several times, and only left me and went away after I had rejected his advice (I was to all intents and purposes gambling drunk) in terms which rendered it impossible for him to address me again that night.

Shortly after he had gone, a hoarse voice behind me cried: "Permit me, my dear sir—permit me to restore to their proper place two **napoleons** which you have dropped. Wonderful luck, sir! I pledge you my word of honour, as an old soldier, in the course of my long experience in this sort of thing, I never saw such luck as yours—never! Go on, sir—*Sacre mille bombes!* Go on boldly, and break the bank!"

I turned round and saw, nodding and smiling at me with **inveterate** civility, a tall man, dressed in a **frogged and braided surtout**.

If I had been in my senses, I should have considered him, personally, as being rather a suspicious specimen of an old soldier. He had goggling, bloodshot eyes, mangy moustaches, and a broken nose. His voice betrayed a **barrack-room intonation** of the worst order, and he had the dirtiest pair of hands I ever saw—even in France. These little personal peculiarities exercised, however, no repelling influence on me. In the mad excitement, the reckless triumph of that moment, I was ready to "**fraternize**" with anybody who encouraged me in my game. I accepted the old soldier's offered pinch of snuff; clapped him on the back, and swore he was the honestest fellow in the world—the most glorious relic of the Grand Army that I had ever met with. "Go on!" cried my military friend, snapping his fingers in ecstasy—"Go on, and win! Break the bank—*Mille tonnerres!* my gallant English comrade, break the bank!"

And I *did* go on—went on at such a rate, that in another quarter of an hour the croupier called out, "Gentlemen, the bank has discontinued for to-night." All the notes, and all the gold in that "bank" now lay in a heap under my hands; the whole floating capital of the gambling-house was waiting to pour into my pockets!

"Tie up the money in your pocket-handkerchief, my worthy sir," said the old soldier, as I wildly plunged my hands into my heap of gold. "Tie it up, as we used to tie up a bit of dinner in the Grand Army; your winnings are too heavy for any breeches-pockets that ever were sewed. There! that's it—shovel them in, notes and all! *Credie!* what luck! Stop! another napoleon on the floor! *Ah! sacre petit polisson de Napoleon!* have I found thee at last? Now then, sir—two tight double knots each way with your honourable permission, and the money's safe. Feel it! feel it, fortunate sir! hard and round as a cannon-ball—*Ah, bah!* if they had only fired such cannon-balls at us at **Austerlitz**—*nom d'une pipe!* if they only had! And now, as an ancient **grenadier**, as an ex-brave of the French army, what remains for me to do? I ask what? Simply this: to **entreat** my valued English friend to drink a bottle of Champagne with me, and toast the goddess Fortune in foaming goblets before we part!"

Excellent ex-brave! **Convivial** ancient grenadier! Champagne by all means! An English cheer for an old soldier! Hurrah! hurrah! Another English cheer for the goddess Fortune! Hurrah! hurrah! hurrah!

"Bravo! the Englishman; the amiable, gracious Englishman, in whose veins circulates the vivacious blood of France! Another glass? *Ah, bah!*—the bottle is empty! Never mind! *Vive le vin!* I, the old soldier, order another bottle, and half a pound of bonbons with it!"

"No, no, ex-brave; never—ancient grenadier! *Your* bottle last time; *my* bottle this. Behold it! Toast away! The French Army! the great Napoleon! the present company! the croupier! the honest croupier's wife and daughters—if he has any! the Ladies generally! everybody in the world!"

By the time the second bottle of Champagne was emptied, I felt as if I had been drinking liquid fire—my brain seemed all aflame. No excess in wine had ever had this effect on me before in my life. Was it the result of a stimulant acting upon my system when I was in a highly excited state? Was my stomach in a particularly disordered condition? Or was the Champagne amazingly strong?

"Ex-brave of the French Army!" cried I, in a mad state of exhilaration, "*I* am on fire! how are *you*? You have set me on fire. Do you hear, my hero of Austerlitz? Let us have a third bottle of Champagne to put the flame out!"

The old soldier wagged his head, rolled his goggle-eyes, until I expected to see them slip out of their sockets; placed his dirty forefinger by the side of his broken nose; solemnly **ejaculated** "Coffee!" and immediately ran off into an inner room.

The word pronounced by the eccentric veteran seemed to have a magical effect on the rest of the company present. With one accord they all rose to depart. Probably they had expected to profit by my intoxication; but finding that my new friend was **benevolently** bent on preventing me from getting dead drunk, had now abandoned all hope of thriving pleasantly on my winnings. Whatever their motive might be, at any rate they went away in a body. When the old soldier returned, and sat down again opposite to me at the table, we had the room to ourselves. I could see the croupier, in a sort of **vestibule** which opened out of it, eating his supper in solitude. The silence was now deeper than ever.

A sudden change, too, had come over the "ex-brave". He assumed a **portentously** solemn look; and when he spoke to me again, his speech was ornamented by no oaths, enforced by no finger-snapping, enlivened by no apostrophes or exclamations.

"Listen, my dear sir," said he, in mysteriously confidential tones—"listen to an old soldier's advice. I have been to the mistress of the house (a very charming woman, with a genius for cookery!) to impress on her the necessity of making us some particularly strong and good coffee. You must drink this coffee in order to get rid of your little amiable **exaltation** of spirits before you think of going home—you *must*, my good and gracious friend! With all that money to take home to-night, it is a sacred duty to yourself to have your wits about you. You are known to be a winner to an enormous extent by several gentlemen present to-night, who, in a certain point of view, are very worthy and excellent fellows; but they are mortal men, my dear sir, and they have their amiable weaknesses. Need I say more? Ah, no, no! you understand me! Now, this is what you must do—send for a **cabriolet** when you feel quite well again—draw up all the windows when you get into it—and tell the driver to take you home only through the large and well-lighted thoroughfares. Do this; and you and your money will be safe. Do this; and to-morrow you will thank an old soldier for giving you a word of honest advice."

Just as the ex-brave ended his oration in very lachrymose tones, the coffee came in, ready poured out in two cups. My attentive friend handed me one of the cups with a bow. I was parched with thirst, and drank it off at a **draught**. Almost instantly afterwards, I was seized with a fit of giddiness, and felt more completely intoxicated than ever. The room whirled round and round furiously; the old soldier seemed to be regularly bobbing up and down before me like the piston of a steam-engine. I was half deafened by a violent singing in my ears; a feeling of utter bewilderment, helplessness, idiocy, overcame me. I rose from my chair, holding on by the table to keep my balance; and stammered out that I felt dreadfully unwell—so unwell that I did not know how I was to get home.

"My dear friend," answered the old soldier—and even his voice seemed to be bobbing up and down as he spoke—"my dear friend, it would be madness to go home in *your* state; you would be sure to lose your money; you might be robbed and murdered with the greatest ease. *I* am going to sleep here; do *you* sleep here, too—they make up **capital** beds in this house—take one; sleep off the effects of the wine, and go home safely with your winnings to-morrow—to-morrow, in broad daylight."

I had but two ideas left: one, that I must never let go hold of my handkerchief full of money; the other, that I must lie down somewhere immediately, and fall off into a comfortable sleep. So I agreed to the proposal about the bed, and took the offered arm of the old soldier, carrying my money with my disengaged hand. Preceded by the croupier, we passed along some passages and up a flight of stairs into the bedroom which I was to occupy. The ex-brave shook me warmly by the hand, proposed that we should breakfast together, and then, followed by the croupier, left me for the night.

I ran to the wash-hand stand; drank some of the water in my jug; poured the rest out, and plunged my face into it; then sat down in a chair and tried to compose myself. I soon felt better. The change for my lungs, from the **fetid** atmosphere of the gambling-room to the cool air of the apartment I now occupied, the almost equally refreshing change for my eyes, from the glaring gaslights of the "salon" to the dim, quiet flicker of one bedroom-candle, aided wonderfully the restorative effects of cold water. The giddiness left me, and I began to feel a little like a reasonable being again. My first thought was of the risk of sleeping all night in a gambling-house; my second, of the still greater risk of trying to get out after the house was closed, and of going home alone at night through the streets of Paris with a large sum of money about me. I had slept in worse places than this on my travels; so I determined to lock, bolt, and barricade my door, and take my chance till the next morning.

Accordingly, I secured myself against all intrusion; looked under the bed, and into the cupboard; tried the fastening of the window; and then, satisfied that I had taken every proper precaution, pulled off my upper clothing, put my light, which was a dim one, on the hearth among a feathery litter of wood-ashes, and got into bed, with the handkerchief full of money under my pillow.

I soon felt not only that I could not go to sleep, but that I could not even close my eyes. I was wide awake, and in a high fever. Every nerve in my body trembled—every one of my senses seemed to be **preternaturally** sharpened. I tossed and rolled, and tried every kind of position, and perseveringly sought out the cold corners of the bed, and all to no purpose. Now I thrust my arms over the clothes; now I poked them under the clothes; now I violently shot my legs straight out down to the bottom of the bed; now I convulsively coiled them up as near my chin as they would go; now I shook out my crumpled pillow, changed it to the cool side, patted it flat, and lay down quietly on my back; now I fiercely doubled it in two, set it up on end, thrust it against the board of the bed, and tried a sitting posture. Every effort was in vain; I groaned with **vexation** as I felt that I was in for a sleepless night.

What could I do? I had no book to read. And yet, unless I found out some method of diverting my mind, I felt certain that I was in the condition to imagine all sorts of horrors; to rack my brain with forebodings of every possible and impossible danger; in short, to pass the night in suffering all conceivable varieties of nervous terror.

I raised myself on my elbow, and looked about the room—which was brightened by a lovely moonlight pouring straight through the window—to see if it contained any pictures or ornaments that I could at all clearly distinguish. While my eyes wandered from wall to wall, a remembrance of Le Maistre's delightful little book, "Voyage autour de ma Chambre," occurred to me. I resolved to imitate the French author, and find occupation and amusement enough to relieve the tedium of my wakefulness, by making a mental inventory of every article of furniture I could see, and by following up to their sources the multitude of associations which even a chair, a table, or a wash-hand stand may be made to call forth.

In the nervous unsettled state of my mind at that moment, I found it much easier to make my inventory than to make my reflections, and thereupon soon gave up all hope of thinking in Le Maistre's fanciful track—or, indeed, of thinking at all. I looked about the room at the different articles of furniture, and did nothing more.

There was, first, the bed I was lying in; a four-post bed, of all things in the world to meet with in Paris—yes, a thoroughly clumsy British four-poster, with the regular top lined with chintz—the regular fringed valance all round—the regular stifling, unwholesome curtains, which I remembered having mechanically drawn back against the posts without particularly noticing the bed when I first got into the room. Then there was the marble-topped wash-hand stand, from which the water I had spilled, in my hurry to pour it out, was still dripping, slowly and more slowly, on to the brick floor. Then two small chairs, with my coat, waistcoat, and trousers flung on them. Then a large elbow-chair covered with dirty-white dimity, with my cravat and shirt collar thrown over the back. Then a chest of drawers with two of the brass handles off, and a tawdry, broken china inkstand placed on it by way of ornament for the top. Then the dressing-table, adorned by a very small looking-glass, and a very large pincushion. Then the window—an unusually large window. Then a dark old picture, which the feeble candle dimly showed me. It was a picture of a fellow in a high Spanish hat, crowned with a plume of towering feathers. A swarthy, sinister ruffian, looking upward, shading his eyes with his hand, and looking intently upward—it might be at some tall gallows at which he was going to be hanged. At any rate, he had the appearance of thoroughly deserving it.

This picture put a kind of **constraint** upon me to look upward too—at the top of the bed. It was a gloomy and not an interesting object, and I looked back at the picture. I counted the feathers in the man's hat—they stood out in relief—three white, two green. I observed the crown of his hat, which was of conical shape, according to the fashion supposed to have been favored by **Guido Fawkes**. I wondered what he was looking up at. It couldn't be at the stars; such a desperado was neither astrologer nor astronomer. It must be at the high gallows, and he was going to be hanged presently. Would the executioner come into possession of his conical crowned hat and plume of feathers? I counted the feathers again—three white, two green.

While I still lingered over this very improving and intellectual employment, my thoughts insensibly began to wander. The moonlight shining into the room reminded me of a certain moonlight night in England— the night after a picnic party in a Welsh valley. Every incident of the drive homeward, through lovely scenery, which the moonlight made lovelier than ever, came back to my remembrance, though I had never given the picnic a thought for years; though, if I had *tried* to recollect it, I could certainly have recalled little or nothing of that scene long past. Of all the wonderful faculties that help to tell us we are immortal, which speaks the sublime truth more eloquently than memory? Here was I, in a strange house of the most suspicious character, in a situation of uncertainty, and even of peril, which might seem to make the cool exercise of my recollection almost out of the question; nevertheless, remembering, quite involuntarily, places, people, conversations, minute circumstances of every kind, which I had thought forgotten forever; which I could not possibly have recalled at will, even under the most favorable **auspices**. And what cause had produced in a moment the whole of this strange, complicated, mysterious effect? Nothing but some rays of moonlight shining in at my bedroom window.

I was still thinking of the picnic—of our merriment on the drive home—of the sentimental young lady who *would* quote "**Childe Harold**" because it was moonlight. I was absorbed by these past scenes and past amusements, when, in an instant, the thread on which my memories hung snapped asunder; my attention immediately came back to present things more vividly than ever, and I found myself, I neither knew why nor wherefore, looking hard at the picture again.

Looking for what?

Good God! the man had pulled his hat down on his brows! No! the hat itself was gone! Where was the conical crown? Where the feathers—three white, two green? Not there! In place of the hat and feathers, what dusky object was it that now hid his forehead, his eyes, his shading hand?

Was the bed moving?

I turned on my back and looked up. Was I mad? drunk? dreaming? giddy again? or was the top of the bed really moving down—sinking slowly, regularly, silently, horribly, right down throughout the whole of its length and breadth—right down upon me, as I lay underneath?

My blood seemed to stand still. A deadly paralysing coldness stole all over me as I turned my head round on the pillow and determined to test whether the bed-top was really moving or not, by keeping my eye on the man in the picture.

The next look in that direction was enough. The dull, black, **frowzy** outline of the **valance** above me was within an inch of being parallel with his waist. I still looked breathlessly. And steadily and slowly—very slowly—I saw the figure, and the line of frame below the figure, vanish, as the valance moved down before it.

I am, constitutionally, anything but timid. I have been on more than one occasion in peril of my life, and have not lost my self-possession for an instant; but when the conviction first settled on my mind that the bed-top was really moving, was steadily and continuously sinking down upon me, I looked up shuddering, helpless, panic-stricken, beneath the hideous machinery for murder, which was advancing closer and closer to suffocate me where I lay.

I looked up, motionless, speechless, breathless. The candle, fully spent, went out; but the moonlight still brightened the room. Down and down, without pausing and without sounding, came the bed-top, and still my panic-terror seemed to bind me faster and faster to the mattress on which I lay—down and down it sank, till the dusty odor from the lining of the canopy came stealing into my nostrils.

At that final moment the instinct of self-preservation startled me out of my trance, and I moved at last. There was just room for me to roll myself sideways off the bed. As I dropped noiselessly to the floor, the edge of the murderous canopy touched me on the shoulder.

Without stopping to draw my breath, without wiping the cold sweat from my face, I rose instantly on my knees to watch the bed-top. I was literally spellbound by it. If I had heard footsteps behind me, I could not have turned round; if a means of escape had been miraculously provided for me, I could not have moved to take advantage of it. The whole life in me was, at that moment, concentrated in my eyes.

It descended—the whole canopy, with the fringe round it, came down—down—close down; so close that there was not room now to squeeze my finger between the bed-top and the bed. I felt at the sides, and discovered that what had appeared to me from beneath to be the ordinary light canopy of a four-post bed was in reality a thick, broad mattress, the substance of which was concealed by the valance and its fringe. I looked up and saw the four posts rising hideously bare. In the middle of the bed-top was a huge wooden screw that had evidently worked it down through a hole in the ceiling, just as ordinary presses are worked down on the substance selected for compression. The frightful apparatus moved without making the faintest noise. There had been no creaking as it came down; there was now not the faintest sound from the room above. Amid a dead and awful silence I beheld before me—in the nineteenth century, and in the civilized capital of France—such a machine for secret murder by suffocation as might have existed in the worst days of the **Inquisition**, in the lonely inns among the **Hartz Mountains**, in the mysterious tribunals of **Westphalia**! Still, as I looked on it, I could not move, I could hardly breathe, but I began to recover the power of thinking, and in a moment I discovered the murderous conspiracy framed against me in all its horror.

My cup of coffee had been drugged, and drugged too strongly. I had been saved from being smothered by having taken an overdose of some narcotic. How I had chafed and fretted at the fever fit which had preserved my life by keeping me awake! How recklessly I had confided myself to the two wretches who had led me into this room, determined, for the sake of my winnings, to kill me in my sleep by the surest and most horrible **contrivance** for secretly accomplishing my destruction! How many men, winners like me, had slept, as I had proposed to sleep, in that bed, and had never been seen or heard of more! I shuddered at the bare idea of it.

But, ere long, all thought was again suspended by the sight of the murderous canopy moving once more. After it had remained on the bed—as nearly as I could guess—about ten minutes, it began to move up again. The villains who worked it from above evidently believed that their purpose was now accomplished. Slowly and silently, as it had descended, that horrible bed-top rose towards its former place. When it reached the upper extremities of the four posts, it reached the ceiling, too. Neither hole nor screw could be seen; the bed became in appearance an ordinary bed again—the canopy an ordinary canopy—even to the most suspicious eyes.

Now, for the first time, I was able to move—to rise from my knees—to dress myself in my upper clothing—and to consider of how I should escape. If I betrayed by the smallest noise that the attempt to suffocate me had failed, I was certain to be murdered. Had I made any noise already? I listened intently, looking towards the door.

No! no footsteps in the passage outside—no sound of a tread, light or heavy, in the room above—absolute silence everywhere. Besides locking and bolting my door, I had moved an old wooden chest against it, which I had found under the bed. To remove this chest (my blood ran cold as I thought of what its contents *might* be!) without making some disturbance was impossible; and, moreover, to think of escaping through the house, now barred up for the night, was sheer insanity. Only one chance was left me—the window. I stole to it on tiptoe.

My bedroom was on the first floor, above an *entresol*, and looked into a back street which you have sketched in your view. I raised my hand to open the window, knowing that on that action hung, by the merest hair-breadth, my chance of safety. They keep vigilant watch in a House of Murder. If any part of the frame cracked, if the hinge creaked, I was a lost man! It must have occupied me at least five minutes, reckoning by time—five *hours*, reckoning by suspense—to open that window. I succeeded in doing it silently—in doing it with all the dexterity of a house-breaker—and then looked down into the street. To leap the distance beneath me would be almost certain destruction! Next, I looked round at the sides of the house. Down the left side ran a thick water-pipe which you have drawn—it passed close by the outer edge of the window. The moment I saw the pipe I knew I was saved. My breath came and went freely for the first time since I had seen the canopy of the bed moving down upon me!

To some men the means of escape which I had discovered might have seemed difficult and dangerous enough—to *me* the prospect of slipping down the pipe into the street did not suggest even a thought of peril. I had always been accustomed, by the practice of gymnastics, to keep up my school-boy powers as a daring and expert climber; and knew that my head, hands, and feet would serve me faithfully in any hazards of ascent or descent. I had already got one leg over the window-sill, when I remembered the handkerchief filled with money under my pillow. I could well have afforded to leave it behind me, but I was revengefully determined that the miscreants of the gambling-house should miss their plunder as well as their victim. So I went back to the bed and tied the heavy handkerchief at my back by my cravat.

Just as I had made it tight and fixed it in a comfortable

place, I thought I heard a sound of breathing outside the door. The chill feeling of horror ran through me again as I listened. No! dead silence still in the passage—I had only heard the night air blowing softly into the room. The next moment I was on the window-sill, and the next I had a firm grip on the water-pipe with my hands and knees.

I slid down into the street easily and quietly, as I thought I should, and immediately set off at the top of my speed to a branch **"Prefecture" of Police**, which I knew was situated in the immediate neighbourhood. A "**Sub-prefect**," and several picked men among his subordinates, happened to be up, maturing, I believe, some scheme for discovering the perpetrator of a mysterious murder which all Paris was talking of just then. When I began my story, in a breathless hurry and in very bad French, I could see that the Sub-prefect suspected me of being a drunken Englishman who had robbed somebody; but he soon altered his opinion as I went on, and before I had anything like concluded, he shoved all the papers before him into a drawer, put on his hat, supplied me with another (for I was bareheaded), ordered a file of soldiers, desired his expert followers to get ready all sorts of tools for breaking open doors and ripping up brick flooring, and took my arm, in the most friendly and familiar manner possible, to lead me with him out of the house. I will venture to say that when the Sub-prefect was a little boy, and was taken for the first time to the play, he was not half as much pleased as he was now at the job in prospect for him at the gambling-house!

Away we went through the streets, the Sub-prefect cross-examining and congratulating me in the same breath as we marched at the head of our formidable *posse comitatus*. **Sentinels** were placed at the back and front of the house the moment we got to it; a tremendous battery of knocks was directed against the door; a light appeared at a window; I was told to conceal myself behind the police—then came more knocks and a cry of "Open in the name of the law!" At that terrible summons bolts and locks gave way before an invisible hand, and the moment after the Sub-prefect was in the passage, confronting a waiter half-dressed and ghastly pale. This was the short dialogue which immediately took place:

"We want to see the Englishman who is sleeping in this house?"

"He went away hours ago."

"He did no such thing. His friend went away; *he* remained. Show us to his bedroom!"

"I swear to you, Monsieur le Sous-prefect, he is not here! he—"

"I swear to you, Monsieur le Garcon, he is. He slept here—he didn't find your bed comfortable—he came to us to complain of it—here he is among my men—and here am I ready to look for a flea or two in his bedstead. Renaudin! (calling to one of the subordinates, and pointing to the waiter), collar that man, and tie his hands behind him. Now, then, gentlemen, let us walk upstairs!"

Every man and woman in the house was secured—the "Old Soldier" the first. Then I identified the bed in which I had slept, and then we went into the room above.

No object that was at all extraordinary appeared in any part of it. The Sub-prefect looked round the place, commanded everybody to be silent, stamped twice on the floor, called for a candle, looked attentively at the spot he had stamped on, and ordered the flooring there to be carefully taken up. This was done in no time. Lights were produced, and we saw a deep raftered cavity between the floor of this room and the ceiling of the room beneath. Through this cavity there ran perpendicularly a sort of case of iron thickly greased; and inside the case appeared the screw, which communicated with the bed-top below. Extra lengths of screw, freshly oiled; levers covered with felt; all the complete upper works of a heavy press— constructed with infernal ingenuity so as to join the fixtures below, and when taken to pieces again, to go into the smallest possible compass—were next discovered and pulled out on the floor. After some little difficulty the Sub-prefect succeeded in putting the machinery together, and, leaving his men to work it, descended with me to the bedroom. The smothering canopy was then lowered, but not so noiselessly as I had seen it lowered. When I mentioned this to the Sub-prefect, his answer, simple as it was, had a terrible significance. "My men," said he, "are working down the bed-top for the first time—the men whose money you won were in better practice."

We left the house in the sole possession of two police agents—every one of the inmates being removed to prison on the spot. The Sub-prefect, after taking down my *"proces verbal"* in his office, returned with me to my hotel to get my passport. "Do you think," I asked, as I gave it to him, "that any men have really been smothered in that bed, as they tried to smother *me*?"

"I have seen dozens of drowned men laid out at the morgue," answered the Sub-prefect, "in whose pocketbooks were found letters stating that they had committed suicide in the Seine, because they had lost everything at the gaming table. Do I know how many of those men entered the same gambling-house that *you* entered? won as *you* won? took that bed as *you* took it? slept in it? were smothered in it? and were privately thrown into the river, with a letter of explanation written by the murderers and placed in their pocket-books? No man can say how many or how few have suffered the fate from which you have escaped. The people of the gambling-house kept their bedstead machinery a secret from *us*—even from the police! The dead kept the rest of the secret for them. Good-night, or rather good-morning, Monsieur Faulkner! Be at my office again at nine o'clock—in the meantime, *au revoir*!"

The rest of my story is soon told. I was examined and reexamined; the gambling-house was strictly searched all through from top to bottom; the prisoners were separately interrogated; and two of the less guilty among them made a confession. I discovered that the Old Soldier was the master of the gambling-house—*justice* discovered that he had been drummed out of the army as a vagabond years ago; that he had been guilty of all sorts of villainies since; that he was in possession of stolen property, which the owners identified; and that he, the croupier, another accomplice, and the woman who had made my cup of coffee, were all in the secret of the bedstead. There appeared some reason to doubt whether the inferior persons attached to the house knew anything of the suffocating machinery; and they received the benefit of that doubt, by being treated simply as thieves and vagabonds. As for the Old Soldier and his two head **myrmidons**, they went to the galleys; the woman who had drugged my coffee was imprisoned for I forget how many years; the regular attendants at the gambling-house were considered "suspicious," and placed under "surveillance"; and I became, for one whole week (which is a long time) the head "lion" in Parisian society. My adventure was dramatized by three illustrious play-makers, but never saw theatrical daylight; for the censorship forbade the introduction on the stage of a correct copy of the gambling-house bedstead.

One good result was produced by my adventure,

which any censorship must have approved: it cured me of ever again trying *"Rouge et Noir"* as an amusement. The sight of a green cloth, with packs of cards and heaps of money on it, will henceforth be forever associated in my mind with the sight of a bed canopy descending to suffocate me in the silence and darkness of the night.

Just as Mr Faulkner pronounced these words he started in his chair, and resumed his stiff, dignified position in a great hurry. "Bless my soul!" cried he, with a comic look of astonishment and vexation, "while I have been telling you what is the real secret of my interest in the sketch you have so kindly given to me, I have altogether forgotten that I came here to sit for my portrait. For the last hour or more I must have been the worst model you ever had to draw from!"

"On the contrary, you have been the best," said I. "I have been trying to catch your likeness; and, while telling your story, you have unconsciously shown me the natural expression I wanted to insure my success."

NOTE BY MRS KERBY

I cannot let this story end without mentioning what the chance saying was which caused it to be told at the farmhouse the other night. Our friend the young sailor, among his other quaint objections to sleeping on shore, declared that he particularly hated four-post beds, because he never slept in one without doubting whether the top might not come down in the night and suffocate him. I thought this chance reference to the distinguishing feature of William's narrative curious enough, and my husband agreed with me. But he says it is scarcely worth while to mention such a trifle in anything so important as a book. I cannot venture, after this, to do more than slip these lines in modestly at the end of the story. If the printer should notice my few last words, perhaps he may not mind the trouble of putting them into some out-of-the-way corner.

five-franc pieces French coins
blackguard wicked man
pasteboard playing card
sou coin
hitherto until this time
imperturbable not easily excitable
entreaties earnest requests
napoleon a French coin
inveterate habitual
frogged and braided surtout a coat covered in ornamental braids
barrack-room intonation speaking like a common soldier
fraternize be friendly, associate
Austerlitz a decisive battle in the Napoleonic Wars
grenadier a soldier armed with grenades
entreat beg
convivial sociable
ejaculated said suddenly
benevolently kindly
vestibule lobby
portentously ominously
exaltation raised spirits, state of extreme happiness
cabriolet horse-drawn carriage

draught a swallow of liquid
capital very good
fetid unpleasant smelling
preternaturally unusually
vexation annoyance
constraint restriction
Guido Fawkes Guy Fawkes
auspices circumstances
Childe Harold a poem by Lord Byron
frowzy scruffy
valance short curtain around the frame of a bed
Inquisition the Spanish Inquisition
Hartz Mountains an area of Germany, associated with the fairy tales collected by the Brothers Grimm
Westphalia a region of Germany
contrivance ingenious device
entresol intermediate floor
"Prefecture" of Police police headquarters
Sub-prefect official
comitatus a band of warriors
sentinels guards or sentries
myrmidon someone who follows orders without question

Science fiction stories

The genre of science fiction came of age in the 19th century. This was a time when scientists were making great discoveries in the fields of physics, chemistry and biology, transforming people's understanding of life on earth and humanity's place in the universe. From Charles Darwin's theory of evolution to the discovery of the power of radioactivity, these achievements inspired many writers to explore the implications of scientific progress at this time in novels and short stories.

Seen by many as the first real science fiction novel, *Frankenstein* by Mary Shelley, first published in 1818, was inspired by scientific experiments into 'galvanism', where electrical currents were applied to the corpses of dead animals and even people. In this novel, Shelley created the character of Victor Frankenstein, a brilliant student who harnesses the power of science in order to create life but instead manufactures a monster.

Mary Shelley explored other science fiction themes in her fiction, including in her novel *The Last Man* which tells the story of a 21st-century earth where humanity is destroyed by a virulent plague which eventually leaves a sole survivor. In her short story included in this collection, 'The Mortal Immortal', Shelley tells the tale of a young man who works as an alchemist's apprentice whose experiments seek to find the key to eternal life and her narrative explores the implications of immortality.

The term 'science fiction' was only coined in the 20th century, but the 19th-century author who invented and popularized many of its themes from time travel to alien invasion was Herbert George Wells. A prolific writer of fiction, H. G. Wells' novels and short stories began to appear in the last decade of the 19th century. In 1895 his novel *The Time Machine* was serialized in *The New Review* magazine and became an instant bestseller, with a revised version of the novel published in book form later in that year. This novel told the story of a Victorian gentleman who invents a time machine and uses this to travel far into the future, reporting on the strange world that he finds there.

From this tale of time travel Wells moved on to write the following novels: *The Island of Doctor Moreau* (1896), a story about a scientist's experiments to create men from beasts; *The Invisible Man* (1897), where the sinister scientist of the title discovers the secret of invisibility; and *The War of the Worlds* (1898), a tale of alien invaders landing from Mars. These groundbreaking novels have been adapted into numerous films, TV series, comic books and radio dramas as well as inspiring countless other authors to write their own science fiction stories.

His short story included in this collection, 'The Star', looks forward to cosmic disaster movies such as *Armageddon* and *Deep Impact*, as Wells describes how the Earth is threatened by a rogue star that sweeps through the solar system.

The Star by H. G. Wells

> *The Star* was first published in the Christmas edition of *The Graphic* magazine in 1897. During the 19th century, advances in science had popularized astronomy, with the discovery of the planet Neptune in 1846 inspiring many people to look to the stars.
>
> **Please note:** this story includes terms that are considered offensive nowadays and should be avoided. They have been retained in this story to reflect the language and attitudes of the time.

It was on the first day of the new year that the announcement was made, almost simultaneously from three observatories, that the motion of the planet Neptune, the outermost of all the planets that wheel about the sun, had become very erratic. Ogilvy had already called attention to a suspected **retardation** in its **velocity** in December. Such a piece of news was scarcely calculated to interest a world the greater portion of whose inhabitants were unaware of the existence of the planet Neptune, nor outside the astronomical profession did the subsequent discovery of a faint remote speck of light in the region of the **perturbed** planet cause any very great excitement. Scientific people, however, found the intelligence remarkable enough, even before it became known that the new body was rapidly growing larger and brighter, that its motion was quite different from the orderly progress of the planets, and that the deflection of Neptune and its satellite was becoming now of an unprecedented kind.

Few people without a training in science can realize the huge isolation of the solar system. The sun with its specks of planets, its dust of planetoids, and its impalpable comets, swims in a vacant immensity that almost defeats the imagination. Beyond the orbit of Neptune there is space, vacant so far as human observation has penetrated, without warmth or light or sound, blank emptiness, for twenty million times a million miles. That is the smallest estimate of the distance to be traversed before the very nearest of the stars is attained. And, saving a few comets more unsubstantial than the thinnest flame, no matter had ever to human knowledge crossed this gulf of space, until early in the twentieth century this strange wanderer appeared. A vast mass of matter it was, bulky, heavy, rushing without warning out of the black mystery of the sky into the radiance of the sun. By the second day it was clearly visible to any decent instrument, as a speck with a barely sensible diameter, in the constellation Leo near Regulus. In a little while an opera-glass could attain it.

On the third day the new year the newspaper readers of two hemispheres were made aware for the first time of the real importance of this unusual apparition in the heavens. 'A Planetary Collision,' one London paper headed the news, and proclaimed Duchaine's opinion that this strange new planet would probably collide with Neptune. The leader writers enlarged upon the topic. So that in most of the capitals of the world, on January 3rd, there was an expectation, however vague, of some imminent phenomenon in the sky; and as the night followed the sunset round the globe, thousands of men turned their eyes skyward to see – the old familiar stars just as they had always been.

Until it was dawn in London and **Pollux** setting and the stars overhead grown pale. The winter's dawn it was, a sickly filtering accumulation of daylight, and the light of gas and candles shone yellow in the windows to show where people were **astir**. But the yawning policeman saw the thing, the busy crowds in the markets stopped agape, workmen going to their work betimes, milkmen, the drivers of news-carts, dissipation going home jaded and pale, homeless wanderers, sentinels on their beats, and in the country, labourers trudging afield, poachers slinking home, all over the dusky quickening country it could be seen – and out at sea by seamen watching for the day – a great white star, come suddenly into the westward sky!

Brighter it was than any star in our skies; brighter than the evening star at its brightest. It still glowed out white and large, no mere twinkling spot of light, but a small round clear shining disc, an hour after the day had come. And where science has not reached, men stared and feared, telling one another of the wars and pestilences that are foreshadowed by these fiery signs in the Heavens. Sturdy **Boers**, dusky **Hottentots**, **Gold Coast Negroes**, Frenchmen, Spaniards, Portuguese, stood in the warmth of the sunrise watching the setting of this strange new star.

And in a hundred observatories there had been suppressed excitement, rising almost to shouting pitch, as the two remote bodies had rushed together, and a hurrying to and fro to gather photographic apparatus and **spectroscope**, and this appliance and that, to record this novel astonishing sight, the destruction of a world. For it was a world, a sister planet of our earth, far greater than our earth indeed, that had so suddenly flashed into flaming death. Neptune it was, had been struck, fairly and squarely, by the strange planet from outer space and the heat of the concussion had incontinently turned two solid globes into one vast mass of incandescence. Round the world that day, two hours before the dawn, went the pallid great white star, fading only as it sank westward and the sun mounted above it. Everywhere men marvelled at it, but of all those who saw it none could have marvelled more than those sailors, habitual watchers of the stars, who far away at sea had heard nothing of its advent and saw it now rise like a pigmy moon and climb **zenithward** and hang overhead and sink westward with the passing of the night.

And when next it rose over Europe everywhere were crowds of watchers on hilly slopes, on house-roofs, in open spaces, staring eastward for the rising of the great new star. It rose with a white glow in front of it, like the glare of a white fire, and those who had seen it come into existence the night before cried out at the sight of it. 'It is larger,' they cried. 'It is brighter!' And, indeed the moon a quarter full and sinking in the west was in its apparent size beyond comparison, but scarcely in all its breadth had it as much brightness now as the little circle of the strange new star.

'It is brighter!' cried the people clustering in the streets. But in the dim observatories the watchers held their breath and peered at one another. 'It is *nearer*,' they said. '*Nearer!*'

And voice after voice repeated, 'It is nearer,' and the clicking telegraph took that up, and it trembled along telephone wires, and in a thousand cities grimy compositors fingered the type. 'It is nearer.' Men writing in offices, struck with a strange realization, flung down their pens; men talking in a thousand places suddenly came upon a grotesque possibility in those words, 'It is nearer.' It hurried along awakening streets, it was shouted down the frost-stilled ways of quiet villages, men who had read these things from the throbbing tape stood in yellow-lit doorways shouting the news to the passers-by. 'It is nearer.' Pretty women, flushed and glittering, heard the news told jestingly between the dances, and feigned an intelligent interest they did not feel. 'Nearer! Indeed. How curious! How very, very clever people must be to find out things like that!'

Lonely tramps faring through the wintry night murmured those words to comfort themselves – looking skyward. 'It has need to be nearer, for the night's as cold as charity. Don't seem much warmth from it if it *is* nearer, all the same.'

'What is a new star to me?' cried the weeping woman kneeling beside her dead.

The schoolboy, rising early for his examination work, puzzled it out for himself – with the great white star, shining broad and bright through the frost-flowers of his window. 'Centrifugal, centripetal,' he said, with his chin on his fist. 'Stop a planet in its flight, rob it of its centrifugal force, what then? Centripetal has it, and down it falls into the sun! And this – !

'Do *we* come in the way? I wonder – '

The light of that day went the way of its brethren, and with the later watches of the frosty darkness rose the strange star again. And it was now so bright that the waxing moon seemed but a pale yellow ghost of itself, hanging huge in the sunset. In a South African City a great man had married, and the streets were alight to welcome his return with his bride. 'Even the skies have illuminated,' said the flatterer. Under Capricorn, two Negro lovers, daring the wild beasts and evil spirits, for love of one another, crouched together in a cane brake where the fireflies hovered. 'That is our star,' they whispered, and felt strangely comforted by the sweet brilliance of its light.

The master mathematician sat in his private room and pushed the papers from him. His calculations were already finished. In a small white phial there still remained a little of the drug that had kept him awake and active for four long nights. Each day, serene, explicit, patient as ever, he had given his lecture to his students, and then had come back at once to this momentous calculation. His face was grave, a little drawn and hectic from his drugged activity. For some time he seemed lost in thought. Then he went to the window, and the blind went up with a click. Half way up the sky, over the clustering roofs, chimneys and steeples of the city, hung the star.

He looked at it as one might look into the eyes of a brave enemy. 'You may kill me,' he said after a silence. 'But I can hold you – and all the universe for that matter – in the grip of this little brain. I would not change. Even now.'

He looked at the little phial. 'There will be no need of sleep again,' he said. The next day at noon, punctual to the minute, he entered his lecture theatre, put his hat on the end of the table as his habit was, and carefully selected a large piece of chalk. It was a joke among his students that he could not lecture without that piece of chalk to fumble in his fingers, and once he had been stricken to impotence by their hiding his supply. He came and looked under his grey eyebrows at the rising tiers of young fresh faces, and spoke with his accustomed studied commonness of phrasing. 'Circumstances have arisen – circumstances beyond my control,' he said and paused, 'which will debar me from completing the course I had designed. It would seem, gentlemen, if I may put the thing clearly and briefly, that – Man has lived in vain.'

The students glanced at one another. Had they heard **aright**? Mad? Raised eyebrows and grinning lips there were, but one or two faces remained intent upon his calm grey-fringed face. 'It will be interesting,' he was saying, 'to devote this morning to an **exposition**, so far as I can make it clear to you, of the calculations that have led me to this conclusion. Let us assume –'

He turned towards the blackboard, meditating a diagram in the way that was usual to him. 'What was that about "lived in vain"?' whispered one student to another. 'Listen,' said the other, nodding towards the lecturer.

And presently they began to understand.

That night the star rose later, for its proper eastward motion had carried it some way across Leo towards Virgo, and its brightness was so great that the sky became a luminous blue as it rose, and every star was hidden in its turn, save only Jupiter near the zenith, Capella, Aldebaran, Sirius and the pointers of the Bear. It was very white and beautiful. In many parts of the world that night a pallid halo encircled it about. It was perceptibly larger; in the clear refractive sky of the tropics it seemed as if it were nearly a quarter the size of the moon. The frost was still on the ground in England, but the world was as brightly lit as if it were midsummer moonlight. One could see to read quite ordinary print by that cold clear light, and in the cities the lamps burnt yellow and wan.

And everywhere the world was awake that night, and throughout Christendom a sombre murmur hung in the keen air over the countryside like the belling of bees in the heather, and this murmurous tumult grew to a **clangour** in the cities. It was the tolling of the bells in a million belfry towers and steeples, summoning the people to sleep no more, to sin no more, but to gather in their churches and pray. And overhead, growing larger and brighter as the earth rolled on its way and the night passed, rose the dazzling star.

And the streets and houses were alight in all the cities, the shipyards glared, and whatever roads led to high country were lit and crowded all night long. And in all the seas about the civilized lands, ships with throbbing engines, and ships with bellying sails, crowded with men and living creatures, were standing out to ocean and the north. For already the warning of the master mathematician had been telegraphed all over the world, and translated into a hundred tongues. The new planet and Neptune, locked in a fiery embrace, were whirling headlong, ever faster and faster towards the sun. Already every second this blazing mass flew a hundred miles, and every second its terrific velocity increased. As it flew now, indeed, it must pass a hundred million of miles wide of the earth and scarcely affect it. But near its destined path, as yet only slightly perturbed, spun the mighty planet Jupiter and his moons sweeping splendid round the sun. Every moment now the attraction between the fiery star and the greatest of the planets grew stronger. And the result of that attraction? Inevitably Jupiter would be deflected from its orbit into an elliptical path, and the burning star, swung by his attraction wide of its sunward rush, would 'describe a curved path' and perhaps collide with, and certainly pass very close to, our earth. 'Earthquakes, volcanic outbreaks, cyclones, sea waves, floods, and a steady rise in temperature to I know not what limit' – so prophesied the master mathematician.

And overhead, to carry out his words, lonely and cold and livid, blazed the star of the coming doom.

To many who stared at it that night until their eyes ached, it seemed that it was visibly approaching. And that night, too, the weather changed, and the frost that had gripped all Central Europe and France and England softened towards a thaw.

But you must not imagine because I have spoken of people praying through the night and people going aboard ships and people fleeing toward mountainous country that the whole world was already in a terror because of the star. As a matter of fact, use and wont still ruled the world, and save for the talk of idle moments and the splendour of the night, nine human beings out of ten were still busy at their common occupations. In all the cities the shops, save one here and there, opened and closed at their proper hours, the doctor and the undertaker plied their trades, the workers gathered in the factories, soldiers drilled, scholars studied, lovers sought one another, thieves lurked and fled, politicians planned their schemes. The presses of the newspapers roared through the nights, and many a priest of this church and that would not open his holy building to further what he considered a foolish panic. The newspapers insisted on the lesson of the year 1000 – for then, too, people had anticipated the end. The star was no star – mere gas – a comet; and were it a star it could not possibly strike the earth. There was no precedent for such a thing. Common sense was sturdy everywhere, scornful, jesting, a little inclined to persecute the obdurate fearful. That night, at seven-fifteen by Greenwich time, the star would be at its nearest to Jupiter. Then the world would see the turn things would take. The master mathematician's grim warnings were treated by many as so much mere elaborate self-advertisement. Common sense at last, a little heated by argument, signified its unalterable convictions by going to bed. So, too, barbarism and savagery, already tired of the novelty, went about their nightly business, and save for a howling dog here and there, the beast world left the star unheeded.

And yet, when at last the watchers in the European States saw the star rise, an hour later it is true, but no larger than it had been the night before, there were still plenty awake to laugh at the master mathematician – to take the danger as if it had passed.

But hereafter the laughter ceased. The star grew – it grew with a terrible steadiness hour after hour, a little larger each hour, a little nearer the midnight zenith, and brighter and brighter, until it had turned night into a second day. Had it come straight to the earth instead of in a curved path, had it lost no velocity to Jupiter, it must have leapt the intervening gulf in a day, but as it was it took five days altogether to come by our planet. The next night it had become a third the size of the moon before it set to English eyes, and the thaw was assured. It rose over America near the size of the moon, but blinding white to look at, and *hot*; and a breath of hot wind blew now with its rising and gathering strength, and in Virginia, and Brazil, and down the **St Lawrence valley**, it shone intermittently through a driving reek of thunder-clouds, flickering violet lightning, and hail unprecedented. In **Manitoba** was a thaw and devastating floods. And upon all the mountains of the earth the snow and ice began to melt that night, and all the rivers coming out of high country flowed thick and turbid, and soon – in their upper reaches – with swirling trees and the bodies of beasts and men. They rose steadily, steadily in the ghostly brilliance, and came trickling over their banks at last, behind the flying population of their valleys.

And along the coast of Argentina and up the South Atlantic the tides were higher than had ever been in the memory of man, and the storms drove the waters in many cases scores of miles inland, drowning whole cities. And so great grew the heat during the night that the rising of the sun was like the coming of a shadow. The earthquakes began and grew until all down America from the Arctic Circle to Cape Horn, hillsides were sliding, fissures were opening, and houses and walls crumbling to destruction. The whole side of **Cotopaxi** slipped out in one vast convulsion, and a tumult of lava poured out so high and broad and swift and liquid that in one day it reached the sea.

So the star, with the wan moon in its wake, marched across the Pacific, trailed the thunderstorms like the hem of a robe, and the growing tidal wave that toiled behind it, frothing and eager, poured over island and island and swept them clear of men. Until that wave came at last – in a blinding light and with the breath of a furnace, swift and terrible it came – a wall of water, fifty feet high, roaring hungrily, upon the long coasts of Asia, and swept inland across the plains of China. For a space the star, hotter now and larger and brighter than the sun in its strength, showed with pitiless brilliance the wide and populous country; towns and villages with their pagodas and trees, roads, wide cultivated fields, millions of sleepless people staring in helpless terror at the incandescent sky; and then, low and growing, came the murmur of the flood. And thus it was with millions of men that night – a flight **nowhither**, with limbs heavy with heat and breath fierce and scant, and the flood like a wall swift and white behind. And then death.

China was lit glowing white, but over Japan and Java and all the islands of Eastern Asia the great star was a ball of dull red fire because of the steam and smoke and ashes the volcanoes were spouting forth to salute its coming. Above was the lava, hot gases and ash, and below the seething floods, and the whole earth swayed and rumbled with the earthquake shocks. Soon the **immemorial** snows of **Tibet** and the Himalaya were melting and pouring down by ten million deepening converging channels upon the plains of **Burma** and **Hindustan**. The tangled summits of the Indian jungles were aflame in a thousand places, and below the hurrying waters around the stems were dark objects that still struggled feebly and reflected the blood-red tongues of fire. And in a rudderless confusion a multitude of men and women fled down the broad river-ways to that one last hope of men – the open sea.

Larger grew the star, and larger, hotter, and brighter with a terrible swiftness now. The tropical ocean had lost its phosphorescence, and the whirling steam rose in ghostly wreaths from the black waves that plunged incessantly, speckled with storm-tossed ships.

And then came a wonder. It seemed to those who in Europe watched for the rising of the star that the world must have ceased its rotation. In a thousand open spaces of down and upland the people who had fled thither from the floods and the falling houses and sliding slopes of hill watched for that rising in vain. Hour followed hour through a terrible suspense, and the star rose not. Once again men set their eyes upon the old constellations they had counted lost to them forever. In England it was hot and clear overhead, though the ground quivered perpetually, but in the tropics, **Sirius** and **Capella** and **Aldebaran** showed through a veil of steam. And when at last the great star rose near ten hours late, the sun rose close upon it, and in the centre of its white heart was a disc of black.

Over Asia it was the star had begun to fall behind

the movement of the sky, and then suddenly, as it hung over India, its light had been veiled. All the plain of India from the mouth of the **Indus** to the mouths of the **Ganges** was a shallow waste of shining water that night, out of which rose temples and palaces, mounds and hills, black with people. Every minaret was a clustering mass of people, who fell one by one into the **turbid** waters, as heat and terror overcame them. The whole land seemed a-wailing and suddenly there swept a shadow across that furnace of despair, and a breath of cold wind, and a gathering of clouds, out of the cooling air. Men looking up, near blinded, at the star, saw that a black disc was creeping across the light. It was the moon, coming between the star and the earth. And even as men cried to God at this respite, out of the East with a strange inexplicable swiftness sprang the sun. And then star, sun and moon rushed together across the heavens.

So it was that presently, to the European watchers, star and sun rose close upon each other, drove headlong for a space and then slower, and at last came to rest, star and sun merged into one glare of flame at the zenith of the sky. The moon no longer eclipsed the star but was lost to sight in the brilliance of the sky. And though those who were still alive regarded it for the most part with that dull stupidity that hunger, fatigue, heat and despair engender, there were still men who could perceive the meaning of these signs. Star and earth had been at their nearest, had swung about one another, and the star had passed. Already it was receding, swifter and swifter, in the last stage of its headlong journey downward into the sun.

And then the clouds gathered, blotting out the vision of the sky, the thunder and lightning wove a garment round the world; all over the earth was such a downpour of rain as men had never before seen, and where the volcanoes flared red against the cloud canopy there descended torrents of mud. Everywhere the waters were pouring off the land, leaving mud-silted ruins, and the earth littered like a storm-worn beach with all that had floated, and the dead bodies of the men and brutes, its children. For days the water streamed off the land, sweeping away soil and trees and houses in the way, and piling huge dykes and scooping out Titanic gullies over the countryside. Those were the days of darkness that followed the star and the heat. All through them, and for many weeks and months, the earthquakes continued.

But the star had passed, and men, hunger-driven and gathering courage only slowly, might creep back to their ruined cities, buried granaries, and sodden fields. Such few ships as had escaped the storms of that time came stunned and shattered and sounding their way cautiously through the new marks and shoals of once familiar ports. And as the storms subsided men perceived that everywhere the days were hotter than of yore, and the sun larger, and the moon, shrunk to a third of its former size, took now fourscore days between its new and new.

But of the new brotherhood that grew presently among men, of the saving of laws and books and machines, of the strange change that had come over Iceland and Greenland and the shores of Baffin's Bay, so that the sailors coming there presently found them green and gracious, and could scarce believe their eyes, this story does not tell. Nor of the movement of mankind now that the earth was hotter, northward and southward towards the poles of the earth. It concerns itself only with the coming and the passing of the Star.

The Martian astronomers – for there are astronomers on Mars, although they are very different beings from men – were naturally profoundly interested by these things. They saw them from their own standpoint of course. 'Considering the mass and temperature of the missile that was flung through our solar system into the sun,' one wrote, 'it is astonishing what a little damage the earth, which it missed so narrowly, has sustained. All the familiar continental markings and the masses of the seas remain intact, and indeed the only difference seems to be a shrinkage of the white discoloration (supposed to be frozen water) round either pole.' Which only shows how small the vastest of human catastrophes may seem, at a distance of a few million miles.

---

retardation delay
velocity speed
perturbed disturbed
Pollux star in the constellation of Gemini
astir in a state of activity
Boers South Africans of Dutch descent
Hottentots (now viewed as a derogatory term) South African tribesmen
Gold Coast Negroes (now viewed as a derogatory term) black people from an area in West Africa
spectroscope a device used to measure light
zenithward towards the highest point
aright correctly
exposition explanatory account of a theory
clangour loud ringing sound
St Lawrence valley a Canadian river
Manitoba a Canadian province
Cotopaxi a volcano in the Andes mountains
nowhither towards no place
immemorial very old
Thibet Tibet
Burma a country in South-East Asia now known as Myanmar
Hindustan a northern region in India
Sirius, Capella, Aldebaran stars
Indus, Ganges rivers in India
turbid muddy

The Mortal Immortal
by Mary Shelley

Written by Mary Shelley in 1833, *The Mortal Immortal* was published in the literary annual *The Keepsake* in 1834. The scientific experiments that gift the narrator his eternal life echo the experiments of Victor Frankenstein in Shelley's earlier novel, *Frankenstein*.

JULY 16, 1833. --This is a memorable anniversary for me; on it I complete my three hundred and twenty-third year!

The Wandering Jew?--certainly not. More than eighteen centuries have passed over his head. In comparison with him, I am a very young Immortal.

Am I, then, immortal? This is a question which I have asked myself, by day and night, for now three hundred and three years, and yet cannot answer it. I detected a gray hair amidst my brown locks this very day--that surely signifies decay. Yet it may have remained concealed there for three hundred years--for some persons have become entirely white headed before twenty years of age.

I will tell my story, and my reader shall judge for me. I will tell my story, and so contrive to pass some few hours of a long eternity, become so wearisome to me. For ever!

Can it be? to live for ever! I have heard of enchantments, in which the victims were plunged into a deep sleep, to wake, after a hundred years, as fresh as ever: I have heard of the **Seven Sleepers**--thus to be immortal would not be so **burthensome**: but, oh! the weight of never-ending time--the tedious passage of the still-succeeding hours! How happy was the fabled **Nourjahad**!----But to my task.

All the world has heard of **Cornelius Agrippa**. His memory is as immortal as his arts have made me. All the world has also heard of his scholar, who, unawares, raised the foul fiend during his master's absence, and was destroyed by him. The report, true or false, of this accident, was attended with many inconveniences to the renowned **philosopher**. All his scholars at once deserted him--his servants disappeared. He had no one near him to put coals on his ever-burning fires while he slept, or to attend to the changeful colours of his medicines while he studied. Experiment after experiment failed, because one pair of hands was insufficient to complete them: the dark spirits laughed at him for not being able to retain a single mortal in his service.

I was then very young--very poor--and very much in love. I had been for about a year the pupil of Cornelius, though I was absent when this accident took place. On my return, my friends implored me not to return to the alchymist's **abode**. I trembled as I listened to the dire tale they told; I required no second warning; and when

Cornelius came and offered me a purse of gold if I would remain under his roof, I felt as if Satan himself tempted me. My teeth chattered--my hair stood on end:--I ran off as fast as my trembling knees would permit.

My failing steps were directed whither for two years they had every evening been attracted,--a gently bubbling spring of pure living waters, beside which lingered a dark-haired girl, whose beaming eyes were fixed on the path I was accustomed each night to tread. I cannot remember the hour when I did not love Bertha; we had been neighbours and playmates from infancy--her parents, like mine, were of humble life, yet respectable --our attachment had been a source of pleasure to them. In an evil hour, a malignant fever carried off both her father and mother, and Bertha became an orphan. She would have found a home beneath my paternal roof, but, unfortunately, the old lady of the near castle, rich, childless, and solitary, declared her intention to adopt her. Henceforth Bertha was clad in silk--inhabited a marble palace--and was looked on as being highly favoured by fortune. But in her new situation among her new associates, Bertha remained true to the friend of her humbler days; she often visited the cottage of my father, and when forbidden to go **thither**, she would stray towards the neighbouring wood, and meet me beside its shady fountain.

She often declared that she owed no duty to her new

protectress equal in **sanctity** to that which bound us. Yet still I was too poor to marry, and she grew weary of being tormented on my account. She had a **haughty** but an impatient spirit, and grew angry at the obstacles that prevented our union. We met now after an absence, and she had been sorely **beset** while I was away; she complained bitterly, and almost reproached me for being poor. I replied hastily,--

"I am honest, if I am poor!--were I not, I might soon become rich!"

This exclamation produced a thousand questions. I feared to shock her by owning the truth, but she drew it from me; and then, casting a look of disdain on me, she said--

"You pretend to love, and you fear to face the Devil for my sake!"

I protested that I had only dreaded to offend her;-- while she dwelt on the magnitude of the reward that I should receive. Thus encouraged-- shamed by her--led on by love and hope, laughing at my late fears, with quick steps and a light heart, I returned to accept the offers of the alchymist, and was instantly installed in my office.

A year passed away. I became possessed of no insignificant sum of money. Custom had banished my fears. In spite of the most painful vigilance, I had never detected the trace of a cloven foot; nor was the studious silence of our abode ever disturbed by demoniac howls.

I still continued my stolen interviews with Bertha, and Hope dawned on me--Hope--but not perfect joy; for Bertha fancied that love and security were enemies, and her pleasure was to divide them in my bosom. Though true of heart, she was somewhat of a **coquette** in manner; and I was jealous as a Turk. She slighted me in a thousand ways, yet would never acknowledge herself to be in the wrong. She would drive me mad with anger, and then force me to beg her pardon. Sometimes she fancied that I was not sufficiently submissive, and then she had some story of a rival, favoured by her protectress. She was surrounded by silk-clad youths--the rich and **gay**--What chance had the sad-robed scholar of Cornelius compared with these?

On one occasion, the philosopher made such large demands upon my time, that I was unable to meet her as I was **wont**. He was engaged in some mighty work, and I was forced to remain, day and night, feeding his furnaces and watching his chemical preparations. Bertha waited for me in vain at the fountain. Her haughty spirit fired at this neglect; and when at last I stole out during the few short minutes allotted to me for slumber, and hoped to be consoled by her, she received me with disdain, dismissed me in scorn, and vowed that any man should possess her hand rather than he who could not be in two places at once for her sake. She would be revenged!--And truly she was. In my dingy retreat I heard that she had been hunting, attended by Albert Hoffer. Albert Hoffer was favoured by her protectress, and the three passed in **cavalcade** before my smoky window. **Methought** that they mentioned my name--it was followed by a laugh of derision, as her dark eyes glanced contemptuously towards my abode.

Jealousy, with all its venom, and all its misery, entered my breast. Now I shed a torrent of tears, to think that I should never call her mine; and, **anon**, I **imprecated** a thousand curses on her **inconstancy**. Yet, still I must stir the fires of the alchymist, still attend on the changes of his unintelligible medicines.

Cornelius had watched for three days and nights, nor closed his eyes. The progress of his **alembics** was slower than he expected: in spite of his anxiety, sleep weighed upon his eyelids. Again and again he threw off drowsiness with more than human energy; again and again it stole away his senses. He eyed his **crucibles** wistfully. "Not ready yet," he murmured; "will another night pass before the work is accomplished? Winzy, you are vigilant--you are faithful--you have slept, my boy-- you slept last night. Look at that glass **vessel**. The liquid it contains is of a soft rose-colour: the moment it begins to change its hue, awaken me--till then I may close my eyes. First, it will turn white, and then emit golden flashes; but wait not till then; when the rose-colour fades, **rouse** me." I scarcely heard the last words, muttered, as they were, in sleep. Even then he did not quite yield to nature. "Winzy, my boy," he again said, "do not touch the vessel --do not put it to your lips; it is a **philter**--a philter to cure love; you would not cease to love your Bertha--beware to drink!"

And he slept. His **venerable** head sunk on his breast, and I scarce heard his regular breathing. For a few minutes I watched the vessel--the rosy hue of the liquid remained unchanged. Then my thoughts wandered --they visited the fountain, and dwelt on a thousand charming scenes never to be renewed--never! Serpents and adders were in my heart as the word "Never!" half formed itself on my lips. False girl!--false and cruel! Never more would she smile on me as that evening she smiled on Albert. Worthless, detested woman! I would not remain unrevenged--she should see Albert expire at her feet--she should die beneath my vengeance. She had smiled in disdain and triumph--she knew my wretchedness and her power. Yet what power had she? --the power of exciting my hate--my utter scorn--my--oh, all but indifference! Could I attain that--could I regard her with careless eyes, transferring my rejected love to one fairer and more true, that were indeed a victory!

A bright flash darted before my eyes. I had forgotten the medicine of the **adept**; I gazed on it with wonder: flashes of admirable beauty, more bright than those which the diamond emits when the sun's rays are on it, glanced from the surface of the liquid; an odour the most fragrant and grateful stole over my sense; the vessel seemed one globe of living radiance, lovely to the eye, and most inviting to the taste. The first thought, instinctively inspired by the grosser sense, was, I will--I must drink. I raised the vessel to my lips. "It will cure me of love--of torture!" Already I had **quaffed** half of the most delicious liquor ever tasted by the palate of man, when the philosopher stirred. I **started**--I dropped the glass--the fluid flamed and glanced along the floor, while I felt Cornelius's **gripe** at my throat, as he shrieked aloud, "Wretch! you have destroyed the labour of my life!"

The philosopher was totally unaware that I had drunk any portion of his drug. His idea was, and I gave a **tacit assent** to it, that I had raised the vessel from curiosity, and that, frighted at its brightness, and the flashes of intense light it gave forth, I had let it fall. I never undeceived him. The fire of the medicine was quenched--the fragrance died away--he grew calm, as a philosopher should under the heaviest trials, and dismissed me to rest.

I will not attempt to describe the sleep of glory and bliss which bathed my soul in paradise during the remaining hours of that memorable night. Words would be faint and shallow types of my enjoyment, or of the gladness that possessed my **bosom** when I woke. I trod air--my thoughts were in heaven. Earth appeared heaven, and my inheritance upon it was to be one trance of delight. "This it is to be cured of love," I thought; "I will see Bertha this day, and she will find her lover cold and regardless: too happy to be disdainful, yet how utterly indifferent to her!"

The hours danced away. The philosopher, secure that he had once succeeded, and believing that he might again, began to concoct the same medicine once more. He was shut up with his books and drugs, and I had a holiday. I dressed myself with care; I looked in an old but polished shield, which served me for a mirror; methought my good looks had wonderfully improved. I hurried beyond the precincts of the town, joy in my soul, the beauty of heaven and earth around me. I turned my steps towards the castle--I could look on its lofty turrets with lightness of heart, for I was cured of love. My Bertha saw me afar off, as I came up the avenue. I know not what sudden impulse animated her bosom, but at the sight, she sprung with a light fawn-like bound down the marble steps, and was **hastening** towards me. But I had been perceived by another person. The old high-born hag, who called herself her protectress, and was her tyrant, had seen me, also; she hobbled, panting, up the terrace; a page, as ugly as herself, held up her train, and fanned her as she hurried along, and stopped my fair girl with a "How, now, my bold mistress? whither so fast? Back to your cage--hawks are abroad!"

Bertha clasped her hands--her eyes were still bent on my approaching figure. I saw the contest. How I abhorred the old crone who checked the kind impulses of my Bertha's softening heart. Hitherto, respect for her rank had caused me to avoid the lady of the castle; now I disdained such trivial considerations. I was cured of love, and lifted above all human fears; I hastened forwards, and soon reached the terrace. How lovely Bertha looked! her eyes flashing fire, her cheeks glowing with impatience and anger, she was a thousand times more graceful and charming than ever--I no longer loved--Oh! no, I adored --worshipped--idolized her!

She had that morning been persecuted, with more than usual vehemence, to consent to an immediate marriage with my rival. She was reproached with the encouragement that she had shown him--she was threatened with being turned out of doors with disgrace and shame. Her proud spirit rose in arms at the threat; but when she remembered the scorn that she had heaped upon me, and how, perhaps, she had thus lost one whom she now regarded as her only friend, she wept with remorse and rage. At that moment I appeared. "O, Winzy!" she exclaimed, "take me to your mother's cot; swiftly let me leave the detested luxuries and wretchedness of this noble dwelling--take me to poverty and happiness."

I clasped her in my arms with transport. The old lady was speechless with fury, and broke forth into **invective** only when we were far on our road to my **natal** cottage. My mother received the fair fugitive, escaped from a gilt cage to nature and liberty, with tenderness and joy; my father, who loved her, welcomed her heartily; it was a day of rejoicing, which did not need the addition of the celestial potion of the alchymist to steep me in delight.

Soon after this eventful day, I became the husband of Bertha. I ceased to be the scholar of Cornelius, but I continued his friend. I always felt grateful to him for having, unawares, procured me that delicious draught of a divine elixir, which, instead of curing me of love (sad cure! solitary and joyless remedy for evils which seem blessings to the memory), had inspired me with courage and resolution, thus winning for me an **inestimable** treasure in my Bertha.

I often called to mind that period of trance-like **inebriation** with wonder. The drink of Cornelius had not fulfilled the task for which he affirmed that it had been prepared, but its effects were more potent and blissful than words can express.

They had faded by degrees, yet they lingered long --and painted life in hues of splendour. Bertha often wondered at my lightness of heart and unaccustomed **gaiety**; for, before, I had been rather serious, or even sad, in my **disposition**. She loved me the better for my cheerful temper, and our days were winged by joy.

Five years afterwards I was suddenly summoned to the bedside of the dying Cornelius. He had sent for me in haste, conjuring my instant presence. I found him stretched on his pallet, enfeebled even to death; all of life that yet remained animated his piercing eyes, and they were fixed on a glass vessel, full of a roseate liquid.

"Behold," he said, in a broken and inward voice, "the vanity of human wishes! a second time my hopes are about to be crowned, a second time they are destroyed. Look at that liquor--you remember five years ago I had prepared the same, with the same success;--then, as now, my thirsting lips expected to taste the immortal elixir-- you dashed it from me! and at present it is too late."

He spoke with difficulty, and fell back on his pillow. I could not help saying,--

"How, revered master, can a cure for love restore you to life?"

A faint smile gleamed across his face as I listened earnestly to his scarcely intelligible answer. "A cure for love and for all things--the Elixir of Immortality. Ah! if now I might drink, I should live for ever!"

As he spoke, a golden flash gleamed from the fluid; a well-remembered fragrance stole over the air; he raised himself, all weak as he was--strength seemed miraculously to re-enter his frame--he stretched forth his hand--a loud explosion startled me--a ray of fire shot up from the elixir, and the glass vessel which contained it was shivered to atoms! I turned my eyes towards the philosopher; he had fallen back--his eyes were glassy-- his features rigid--he was dead!

But I lived, and was to live for ever! So said the unfortunate alchymist, and for a few days I believed his words. I remembered the glorious drunkenness that had followed my stolen draught. I reflected on the change I had felt in my frame--in my soul. The bounding elasticity of the one--the buoyant lightness of the other. I surveyed myself in a mirror, and could perceive no change in my features during the space of the five years which had elapsed. I remembered the radiant hues and grateful scent of that delicious beverage--worthy the gift it was capable of bestowing----I was, then, IMMORTAL!

A few days after I laughed at my credulity. The old proverb, that "a prophet is least regarded in his own country," was true with respect to me and my defunct master. I loved him as a man--I respected him as a sage --but I derided the notion that he could command the powers of darkness, and laughed at the superstitious fears with which he was regarded by the vulgar. He was a wise philosopher, but had no acquaintance with any spirits but those clad in flesh and blood. His science was simply human; and human science, I soon persuaded myself, could never conquer nature's laws so far as to imprison the soul for ever within its **carnal habitation**. Cornelius had brewed a soul-refreshing drink--more inebriating than wine--sweeter and more fragrant than any fruit: it possessed probably strong medicinal powers, imparting gladness to the heart and vigor to the limbs; but its effects would wear out; already were they diminished in my frame. I was a lucky fellow to have quaffed health and joyous spirits, and perhaps long life, at my master's hands; but my good fortune ended there: longevity was far different from immortality.

I continued to entertain this belief for many years. Sometimes a thought stole across me--Was the alchymist indeed deceived? But my habitual credence was, that I should meet the fate of all the **children of Adam** at my appointed time--a little late, but still at a natural age. Yet it was certain that I retained a wonderfully youthful look. I was laughed at for my vanity in consulting the mirror so often, but I consulted it in vain--my brow was **untrenched**--my cheeks--my eyes--my whole person continued as untarnished as in my twentieth year.

I was troubled. I looked at the faded beauty of Bertha --I seemed more like her son. By degrees our neighbours began to make similar observations, and I found at last that I went by the name of the Scholar bewitched. Bertha herself grew uneasy. She became jealous and peevish, and at length she began to question me. We had no children; we were all in all to each other; and though, as she grew older, her vivacious spirit became a little allied to ill-temper, and her beauty sadly diminished, I cherished her in my heart as the mistress I had idolized, the wife I had sought and won with such perfect love.

At last our situation became intolerable: Bertha was

fifty--I twenty years of age. I had, in very shame, in some measure adopted the habits of a more advanced age; I no longer mingled in the dance among the young and gay, but my heart bounded along with them while I restrained my feet; and a sorry figure I cut among the **Nestors** of our village. But before the time I mention, things were altered --we were universally shunned; we were--at least, I was --reported to have kept up an **iniquitous** acquaintance with some of my former master's supposed friends. Poor Bertha was pitied, but deserted. I was regarded with horror and **detestation**.

What was to be done? we sat by our winter fire--poverty had made itself felt, for none would buy the produce of my farm; and often I had been forced to journey twenty miles, to some place where I was not known, to dispose of our property. It is true we had saved something for an evil day--that day was come.

We sat by our lone fireside--the old-hearted youth and his **antiquated** wife. Again Bertha insisted on knowing the truth; she **recapitulated** all she had ever heard said about me, and added her own observations. She conjured me to cast off the spell; she described how much more **comely** grey hairs were than my chestnut locks; she **descanted** on the reverence and respect due to age--how preferable to the slight regard paid to mere children: could I imagine that the despicable gifts of youth and good looks outweighed disgrace, hatred, and scorn? Nay, in the end I should be burnt as a dealer in the **black art**, while she, to whom I had not **deigned** to communicate any portion of my good fortune, might be stoned as my accomplice. At length she **insinuated** that I must share my secret with her, and **bestow** on her like benefits to those I myself enjoyed, or she would denounce me--and then she burst into tears.

Thus beset, methought it was the best way to tell the truth. I revealed it as tenderly as I could, and spoke only of a very long life, not of immortality--which representation, indeed, coincided best with my own ideas. When I ended, I rose and said,

"And now, my Bertha, will you denounce the lover of your youth? --You will not, I know. But it is too hard, my poor wife, that you should suffer from my ill-luck and the **accursed arts** of Cornelius. I will leave you--you have wealth enough, and friends will return in my absence. I will go; young as I seem, and strong as I am, I can work and gain my bread among strangers, unsuspected and unknown. I loved you in youth; God is my witness that I would not desert you in age, but that your safety and happiness require it."

I took my cap and moved towards the door; in a moment Bertha's arms were round my neck, and her lips were pressed to mine. "No, my husband, my Winzy," she said, "you shall not go alone--take me with you; we will remove from this place, and, as you say, among strangers we shall be unsuspected and safe. I am not so very old as quite to shame you, my Winzy; and I dare say the charm will soon wear off, and, with the blessing of God, you will become more elderly-looking, as is fitting; you shall not leave me."

I returned the good soul's embrace heartily. "I will not, my Bertha; but for your sake I had not thought of such a thing. I will be your true, faithful husband while you are spared to me, and do my duty by you to the last."

The next day we prepared secretly for our **emigration**. We were obliged to make great **pecuniary** sacrifices--it could not be helped. We **realised** a sum sufficient, at least, to maintain us while Bertha lived; and, without saying **adieu** to any one, quitted our native country to take refuge in a remote part of western France.

It was a cruel thing to transport poor Bertha from her native village, and the friends of her youth, to a new country, new language, new customs. The strange secret of my destiny rendered this removal **immaterial** to me; but I **compassionated** her deeply, and was glad to perceive that she found compensation for her misfortunes in a variety of little ridiculous circumstances. Away from all **tell-tale chroniclers**, she sought to decrease the apparent disparity of our ages by a thousand feminine arts--rouge, youthful dress, and assumed juvenility of manner. I could not be angry-- Did not I myself wear a mask? Why quarrel with hers, because it was less successful? I grieved deeply when I remembered that this was my Bertha, whom I had loved so fondly, and won with such transport--the dark eyed, dark-haired girl, with smiles of enchanting archness and a step like a fawn--this mincing, simpering, jealous old woman. I should have revered her gray locks and withered cheeks; but thus!----It was my, work, I knew; but I did not the less deplore this type of human weakness.

Her jealousy never slept. Her chief occupation was to discover that, in spite of outward appearances, I was myself growing old. I verily believe that the poor soul loved me truly in her heart, but never had woman so tormenting a mode of displaying fondness. She would discern wrinkles in my face and **decrepitude** in my walk, while I bounded along in youthful vigour, the youngest looking of twenty youths. I never dared address another woman: on one occasion, fancying that the belle of the village regarded me with favouring eyes, she bought me a gray wig. Her constant discourse among her acquaintances was, that though I looked so young, there was ruin at work within my frame; and she affirmed that the worst symptom about me was my apparent health. My youth was a disease, she said, and I ought at all times to prepare, if not for a sudden and awful death, at least to awake some morning white-headed, and bowed down with all the marks of advanced years. I let her talk--I often joined in her conjectures. Her warnings chimed in with my never-ceasing speculations concerning my state, and I took an earnest, though painful, interest in listening to all that her quick wit and excited imagination could say on the subject.

Why dwell on these minute circumstances? We lived on for many long years. Bertha became bed-rid and paralytic: I nursed her as mother might a child. She grew peevish, and still **harped upon one string**--of how long I should survive her. It has ever been a source of consolation to me, that I performed my duty scrupulously towards her. She had been mine in youth, she was mine in age, and at last, when I heaped the **sod** over her corpse, I wept to feel that I had lost all that really bound me to humanity.

Since then how many have been my cares and woes, how few and empty my enjoyments! I pause here in my history--I will pursue it no further. A sailor without rudder or compass, tossed on a stormy sea--a traveller lost on a wide-spread heath, without landmark or star to him--such have I been: more lost, more hopeless than either. A nearing ship, a gleam from some far cot, may save them; but I have no beacon except the hope of death.

Death! mysterious, **ill-visaged** friend of weak humanity! Why alone of all mortals have you cast me from your sheltering fold? O, for the peace of the grave! the deep silence of the iron-bound tomb! that thought would cease to work in my brain, and my heart beat no more with emotions varied only by new forms of sadness!

Am I immortal? I return to my first question. In the first place, is it not more probable that the beverage of the alchymist was fraught rather with longevity than eternal life? Such is my hope. And then be it remembered that I only drank half of the potion prepared by him. Was not the whole necessary to complete the charm? To have drained half the Elixir of Immortality is but to be half immortal--my For-ever is thus truncated and null.

But again, who shall number the years of the half of eternity? I often try to imagine by what rule the infinite may be divided. Sometimes I fancy age advancing upon me. One gray hair I have found. Fool! Do I lament? Yes, the fear of age and death often creeps coldly into my heart; and the more I live, the more I dread death, even while I abhor life. Such an enigma is man--born to perish--when he wars, as I do, against the established laws of his nature.

But for this **anomaly** of feeling surely I might die: the medicine of the alchymist would not be proof against fire--sword--and the strangling waters. I have gazed upon the blue depths of many a placid lake, and the tumultuous rushing of many a mighty river, and have said, peace inhabits those waters; yet I have turned my steps away, to live yet another day. I have asked myself, whether suicide would be a crime in one to whom thus only the portals of the other world could be opened. I have done all, except presenting myself as a soldier or duellist, an object of destruction to my--no, not my fellow-mortals, and therefore I have shrunk away. They are not my fellows. The inextinguishable power of life in my frame, and their **ephemeral** existence, place us wide as the poles asunder. I could not raise a hand against the meanest or the most powerful among them.

Thus I have lived on for many a year--alone, and weary of myself--desirous of death, yet never dying--a mortal immortal. Neither ambition nor avarice can enter my mind, and the ardent love that gnaws at my heart, never to be returned--never to find an equal on which to expend itself--lives there only to torment me.

This very day I conceived a design by which I may end all--without self-slaughter, without making another man a **Cain**--an expedition, which mortal frame can never survive, even endued with the youth and strength that inhabits mine. Thus I shall put my immortality to the test, and rest for ever--or return, the wonder and benefactor of the human species.

Before I go, a miserable vanity has caused me to pen these pages. I would not die, and leave no name behind. Three centuries have passed since I quaffed the fatal beverage: another year shall not elapse before, encountering gigantic dangers--warring with the powers of frost in their home--beset by famine, toil, and tempest --I yield this body, too tenacious a cage for a soul which thirsts for freedom, to the destructive elements of air and water--or, if I survive, my name shall be recorded as one of the most famous among the sons of men; and, my task achieved, I shall adopt more resolute means, and, by scattering and annihilating the atoms that compose my frame, set at liberty the life imprisoned within, and so cruelly prevented from soaring from this dim earth to a sphere more congenial to its immortal essence.

Wandering Jew a fictional figure from medieval legend who was supposedly cursed by Jesus to walk the earth until the Second Coming
Seven Sleepers legend of a group of youths who slept for 180 years
burthensome burdensome
Nourjahad a man who is tricked to believe he is immortal
Cornelius Agrippa German alchemist who lived between 1486 and 1535
philosopher a medieval term for an alchemist
abode the place where someone lives
thither to that place
sanctity holiness
haughty proud and arrogant
beset troubled
coquette a woman who flirts
gay cheerful
wont in the habit of doing something, accustomed
cavalcade procession
methought it seemed to me
anon soon
imprecated uttered
inconstancy fickleness, quick to change
alembic an alchemical device used to distil chemicals
crucible container in which metals or other substances may be melted or heated to very high temperatures
vessel container
rouse wake
philter potion
venerable old
adept a person who has attained a high level of skill and knowledge in a specific subject or discipline
quaffed drank
started moved suddenly in surprise
gripe grasp

tacit assent unstated agreement
bosom centre of emotion
hastening hurrying
invective abusive words
natal relating to a person's birth
inestimable too great to be estimated
inebriation drunkenness
gaiety cheerfulness
disposition a person's nature or qualities
carnal habitation living body
children of Adam archaic phrase meaning mankind (i.e. children of the biblical figures Adam and Eve)
untrenched unlined
Nestors wise old men
iniquitous wicked
detestation extreme dislike
antiquated aged, old
recapitulated repeated
comely good-looking
descanted commented
black art black magic
deigned condescended, decided
insinuated hinted unpleasantly
bestow present someone with a gift
accursed arts black magic
emigration the process by which people from one country go and live in other countries
pecuniary financial
realised obtained money in exchange for something by selling it
adieu goodbye
immaterial does not matter at all
compassionated pitied or had compassion for
tell-tale chroniclers gossips
decrepitude the state of being old and feeble
harp on one string dwell on one subject
sod piece of turf, earth
ill-visaged having a harmful appearance
anomaly something that doesn't follow the general rule
ephemeral lasting only a short time
Cain the biblical figure Cain, the first murderer, who killed his brother Abel

Fantasy stories

Fantasy is a genre with a long history, stretching back to the myths and legends of the ancient world. From the dragon in the Old English poem *Beowulf* to the fairies and wizards that can be found in Shakespeare's plays *A Midsummer's Night Dream* and *The Tempest*, concepts and characters associated with this genre can be found throughout English literature. In the 19th century, numerous authors drew on elements of the fantastic in their fiction, shaping the genre in different ways.

In the first half of the century in Germany, the Brothers Grimm collected and published traditional folk stories and fairy tales, establishing the popular versions of stories such as *Cinderella* and *Hansel and Gretel* that we know today. These cautionary tales wove together magical characters such as witches and fairies into dark stories that weren't originally intended for an audience of children.

Later writers such as Oscar Wilde drew on the fairy tale form to craft their own tales of the fantastic. In his short story collections, *The Happy Prince and Other Tales* and *A House of Pomegranates*, Wilde created tales of giants and talking animals to explore the morals of the age. In the short story included in this collection, 'The Star-

Child', Wilde presents the tale of a 'Star-Child' adopted by a woodcutter and his wife and the painful lessons the 'Star-Child' has to learn because of his vanity and selfishness.

Other 19th century writers such as George MacDonald and William Morris helped to establish several conventions of the fantasy genre, such as the creation of imaginary worlds in which their stories were set. George MacDonald's novel *Phantastes*, first published in 1858, describes how his hero travels to a magical land and the quest that he follows there, influencing later 20th-century fantasy writers such as J. R. R. Tolkien and C. S. Lewis.

The 19th century was also an age of adventure, when explorers travelled to previously uncharted areas of the world. As these explorers brought back reports of strange new lands and creatures, authors such as H. Rider Haggard created stories of lost civilizations and ancient magic, mixing fantasy and adventure in his novel, *She*, first published in *The Graphic* magazine from October 1886 to January 1887.

In the second story included in this section, 'The Lizard' by C. J. Cutcliffe Hyne, fantasy intrudes on the real world as a cave explorer discovers an ancient monster which has lain undisturbed for millions of years.

The Star-Child by Oscar Wilde

The Star-Child first appeared in *A House of Pomegranates*, a collection of fairy tales by Oscar Wilde which was published in 1891. Although by this time the fairy tale was seen as a form of writing produced exclusively for children, Oscar Wilde himself stated that this collection was "intended neither for the British child nor the British public".

Once upon a time two poor Woodcutters were making their way home through a great pine-forest. It was winter, and a night of bitter cold. The snow lay thick upon the ground, and upon the branches of the trees: the frost kept snapping the little twigs on either side of them, as they passed: and when they came to the Mountain-Torrent she was hanging motionless in air, for the Ice-King had kissed her.

So cold was it that even the animals and the birds did not know what to make of it.

'Ugh!' snarled the Wolf, as he limped through the brushwood with his tail between his legs, 'this is perfectly monstrous weather. Why doesn't the Government look to it?'

'Weet! weet! weet! twittered the green **Linnets**, 'the

old Earth is dead and they have laid her out in her white shroud.'

'The Earth is going to be married, and this is her bridal dress,' whispered the Turtle-doves to each other. Their little pink feet were quite frost-bitten, but they felt that it was their duty to take a romantic view of the situation.

'Nonsense!' growled the Wolf. 'I tell you that it is all the fault of the Government, and if you don't believe me I shall eat you.' The Wolf had a thoroughly practical mind, and was never at a loss for a good argument.

'Well, for my own part, said the Woodpecker, who was a born philosopher, 'I don't care an atomic theory for explanations. If a thing is so, it is so, and at present it is terribly cold.'

Terribly cold it certainly was. The little Squirrels, who lived inside the tall fir-tree, kept rubbing each other's noses to keep themselves warm, and the Rabbits curled themselves up in their holes, and did not venture even to look out of doors. The only people who seemed to enjoy it were the great horned Owls. Their feathers were quite stiff with rime, but they did not mind, and they rolled their large yellow eyes, and called out to each other across the forest, 'Tu-whit! Tu-whoo! Tu-whit! Tu-whoo! what delightful weather we are having!'

On and on went the two Woodcutters, blowing **lustily** upon their fingers, and stamping with their huge iron-shod boots upon the caked snow. Once they sank into a deep drift, and came out as white as millers are, when the stones are grinding; and once they slipped on the hard smooth ice where the marsh-water was frozen, and their **faggots** fell out of their bundles, and they had to pick them up and bind them together again; and once they thought that they had lost their way, and a great terror seized on them, for they knew that the Snow is cruel to those who sleep in her arms. But they put their trust in the good Saint Martin, who watches over all travellers, and retraced their steps, and went warily, and at last they reached the outskirts of the forest, and saw, far down in the valley beneath them, the lights of the village in which they dwelt.

So overjoyed were they at their **deliverance** that they laughed aloud, and the Earth seemed to them like a flower of silver, and the Moon like a flower of gold.

Yet, after that they had laughed they became sad, for they remembered their poverty, and one of them said to the other, 'Why did we make merry, seeing that life is for the rich, and not for such as we are? Better that we had died of cold in the forest, or that some wild beast had fallen upon us and slain us.'

'Truly,' answered his companion, much is given to some, and little is given to others. Injustice has parcelled out the world, nor is there equal division of **aught** save of sorrow.'

But as they were **bewailing** their misery to each other

this strange thing happened. There fell from heaven a very bright and beautiful star. It slipped down the side of the sky, passing by the other stars in its course, and, as they watched it wondering, it seemed to them to sink behind a clump of willow-trees that stood hard by a little sheep-fold no more than a stone's throw away.

'Why! there is a crook of gold for whoever finds it,' they cried, and they set to and ran, so eager were they for the gold.

And one of them ran taster than his mate, and **outstripped** him, and forced his way through the willows, and came out on the other side, and lo! there was indeed a thing of gold lying on the white snow. So he hastened towards it, and stooping down placed his hands upon it, and it was a cloak of golden tissue, curiously wrought with stars, and wrapped in many folds. And he cried out to his comrade that he had found the treasure that had fallen from the sky, and when his comrade had come up, they sat them down in the snow, and loosened the folds of the cloak that they might divide the pieces of gold. But, alas! no gold was in it, nor silver, nor, indeed, treasure of any kind, but only a little child who was asleep.

And one of them said to the other: 'This is a bitter ending to our hope, nor have we any good fortune, for what doth a child profit to a man? Let us leave it here, and go our way, seeing that we are poor men, and have children of our own whose bread we may not give to another.'

But his companion answered him: 'Nay, but it were an evil thing to leave the child to perish here in the snow, and though I am as poor as **thou art**, and have many mouths to feed, and but little in the pot, yet will I bring it home with me, and my wife shall have care of it.'

So very tenderly he took up the child, and wrapped the cloak around it to shield it from the harsh cold, and made his way down the hill to the village, his comrade marvelling much at his foolishness and softness of heart.

And when they came to the village, his comrade said to him, '**Thou hast** the child, therefore give me the cloak, for it is **meet** that we should share.'

But he answered him: 'Nay, for the cloak is neither mine nor thine, but the child's only,' and he bade him **Godspeed**, and went to his own house and knocked.

And when his wife opened the door and saw that her husband had returned safe to her, she put her arms round his neck and kissed him, and took from his back the bundle of faggots, and brushed the snow off his boots, and bade him come in.

But he said to her, 'I have found something in the forest, and I have brought it to **thee** to have care of it,' and he stirred not from the threshold.

'What is it?' she cried. 'Show it to me, for the house is

bare, and we have need of many things.' And he drew the cloak back, and showed her the sleeping child.

'**Alack**, goodman!' she murmured, 'have we not children enough of our own, that thou must needs bring a **changeling** to sit by the hearth? And who knows if it will not bring us bad fortune? And how shall we tend it?' And she was **wroth** against him.

'Nay, but it is a Star-Child,' he answered; and he told her the strange manner of the finding of it.

But she would not be appeased, but mocked at him, and spoke angrily, and cried: 'Our children lack bread, and shall we feed the child of another? Who is there who **careth** for us? And who **giveth** us food?'

'Nay, but God careth for the sparrows even, and **feedeth** them,' he answered.

'Do not the sparrows die of hunger in the winter?' she asked. And is it not winter now?'

And the man answered nothing, but stirred not from the threshold.

And a bitter wind from the forest came in through the open door, and made her tremble, and she shivered, and said to him: 'Wilt thou not close the door? There **cometh** a bitter wind into the house, and I am cold.'

'Into a house where a heart is hard cometh there not always a bitter wind?' he asked. And the woman answered him nothing, but crept closer to the fire.

And after a time she turned round and looked at him,

and her eyes were full of tears. And he came in swiftly, and placed the child in her arms, and she kissed it, and laid it in a little bed where the youngest of their own children was lying. And on the **morrow** the Woodcutter took the curious cloak of gold and placed it in a great chest, and a chain of amber that was round the child's neck his wife took and set it in the chest also.

So the Star-Child was brought up with the children of the Woodcutter, and sat at the same board with them, and was their playmate. And every year he became more beautiful to look at, so that all those who dwelt in the village were filled with wonder, for, while they were swarthy and black-haired, he was white and delicate as sawn ivory, and his curls were like the rings of the daffodil. His lips, also, were like the petals of a red flower, and his eyes were like violets by a river of pure water, and his body like the **narcissus** of a field where the mower comes not.

Yet did his beauty work him evil. For he grew proud, and cruel, and selfish. The children of the Woodcutter, and the other children of the village, he despised, saying that they were of mean parentage, while he was noble, being sprang from a Star, and he made himself master over them, and called them his servants. No pity had he for the poor, or for those who were blind or maimed or in any way afflicted, but would cast stones at them and drive them forth on to the highway, and bid them beg their bread elsewhere, so that none save the outlaws came twice to that village to ask for alms. Indeed, he was as one **enamoured** of beauty, and would mock at the weakly and ill-favoured, and make jest of them; and himself he loved, and in summer, when the winds were still, he would lie by the well in the priest's orchard and look down at the marvel of his own face, and laugh for the pleasure he had in his fairness.

Often did the Woodcutter and his wife **chide** him, and say: 'We did not deal with thee as thou **dealest** with those who are left desolate, and have none to succour them. **Wherefore art thou** so cruel to all who need pity?'

Often did the old priest send for him, and seek to teach him the love of living things, saying to him: 'The fly is thy brother. Do it no harm. The wild birds that roam through the forest have their freedom. Snare them not for thy pleasure. God made the blind-worm and the mole, and each has its place. Who art thou to bring pain into God's world? Even the cattle of the field praise Him.'

But the Star-Child heeded not their words, but would frown and flout, and go back to his companions, and lead them. And his companions followed him, for he was fair, and fleet of foot, and could dance, and pipe, and make music. And wherever the Star-Child led them they followed, and whatever the Star-Child **bade** them do, that did they. And when he pierced with a sharp reed the dim eyes of the mole, they laughed, and when he cast stones at the leper they laughed also. And in all things he ruled them, and they became hard of heart, even as he was.

Now there passed one day through the village a poor beggar-woman. Her garments were torn and ragged, and her feet were bleeding from the rough road on which she had travelled, and she was in very evil plight. And being weary she sat her down under a chestnut-tree to rest.

But when the Star-Child saw her, he said to his companions, 'See! There **sitteth** a foul beggar-woman under that fair and green-leaved tree. Come, let us drive her hence, for she is ugly and **ill-favoured**.'

So he came near and threw stones at her, and mocked her, and she looked at him with terror in her eyes, nor did she move her gaze from him. And when the Woodcutter, who was **cleaving** logs in a **haggard** hard by, saw what the Star-Child was doing, he ran up and rebuked him, and said to him: 'Surely thou art hard of heart and **knowest** not mercy, for what evil has this poor woman done to thee that thou shouldst treat her in this wise?'

And the Star-Child grew red with anger, and stamped his foot upon the ground, and said, 'Who art thou to question me what I do? I am no son of **thine** to do thy bidding.'

'Thou speakest truly,' answered the Woodcutter, 'yet did I show thee pity when I found thee in the forest.'

And when the woman heard these words she gave a loud cry, and fell into a swoon. And the Woodcutter carried her to his own house, and his wife had care of her, and when she rose up from the swoon into which she had fallen, they set meat and drink before her, and bade her have comfort.

But she would neither eat nor drink, but said to the Woodcutter, 'Didst thou not say that the child was found in the forest? And was it not ten years from this day?'

And the Woodcutter answered, 'Yea, it was in the forest that I found him, and it is ten years from this day.'

'And what signs didst thou find with him?' she cried. 'Bare he not upon his neck a chain of amber? Was not round him a cloak of gold tissue broidered with stars?'

'Truly,' answered the Woodcutter, 'it was even as thou **sayest**.' And he took the cloak and the amber chain from the chest where they lay, and showed them to her.

And when she saw them she wept for joy, and said, 'He is my little son whom I lost in the forest. I pray thee send for him quickly, for in search of him have I wandered over the whole world.'

So the Woodcutter and his wife went out and called to the Star-Child, and said to him, 'Go into the house, and there **shalt** thou find thy mother, who is waiting for thee.'

So he ran in, filled with wonder and great gladness. But when he saw her who was waiting there, he laughed scornfully and said, 'Why, where is my mother? For I see none here but this vile beggar-woman.'

And the woman answered him, 'I am thy mother.'

'Thou art mad to say so,' cried the Star-Child angrily. 'I am no son of thine, for thou art a beggar, and ugly, and in rags. Therefore get thee hence, and let me see thy foul face no more.'

'Nay, but thou art indeed my little son, whom I **bare** in the forest,' she cried, and she fell on her knees, and held out her arms to him. 'The robbers stole thee from me, and left thee to die,' she murmured, 'but I recognized thee when I saw thee, and the signs also have I recognized, the cloak of golden tissue and the amber-chain. Therefore I pray thee come with me, for over the whole world have I wandered in search of thee. Come with me, my son, for I have need of thy love.'

But the Star-Child stirred not from his place, but shut the doors of his heart against her, nor was there any sound heard save the sound of the woman weeping for pain.

And at last he spoke to her, and his voice was hard and bitter. 'If in very truth thou art my mother,' he said, 'it had been better hadst thou stayed away, and not come here to bring me to shame, seeing that I thought I was the child of some Star and not a beggar's child, as thou tellest me that I am. Therefore get thee **hence**, and let me see thee no more.'

'Alas! my son,' she cried, 'wilt thou not kiss me before I go? For I have suffered much to find thee.'

'Nay,' said the Star-Child, 'but thou art too foul to look at and rather would I kiss the adder or the toad than thee.'

So the woman rose up, and went away into the forest weeping bitterly, and when the Star-Child saw that she had gone, he was glad, and ran back to his playmates that he might play with them.

But when they **beheld** him coming, they mocked him and said, 'Why, thou art as foul as the toad, and as loathsome as the adder. Get thee hence, for we will not suffer thee to play with us,' and they **drave** him out of the garden.

And the Star-Child frowned and said to himself, 'What is this that they say to me? I will go to the well of water and look into it, and it shall tell me of my beauty.'

So he went to the well of water and looked into it, and lo! his face was as the face of a toad, and his body was scaled like an adder. And he flung himself down on the grass and wept, and said to himself, 'Surely this has come upon me by reason of my sin. For I have denied my mother, and driven her away, and been proud, and cruel to her. Wherefore I will go and seek her through the whole world, nor will I rest till I have found her.'

And there came to him the little daughter of the Woodcutter, and she put her hand upon his shoulder and said, 'What doth it matter if thou hast lost thy comeliness? Stay with us, and I will not mock at thee.'

And he said to her, 'Nay, but I have been cruel to

my mother, and as a punishment has this evil been sent to me. Wherefore I must go hence, and wander through the world till I find her, and she give me her forgiveness.'

So he ran away into the forest and called out to his mother to come to him, but there was no answer. All day long he called to her, and when the sun set he lay down to sleep on a bed of leaves, and the birds and the animals fled from him, as they remembered his cruelty, and he was alone save for the toad that watched him, and the slow adder that crawled past.

And in the morning he rose up, and plucked some bitter berries from the trees and ate them, and took his way through the great wood, weeping sorely. And of everything that he met he made enquiry if **perchance** they had seen his mother.

He said to the Mole, 'Thou **canst** go beneath the earth. Tell me, is my mother there?'

And the Mole answered, 'Thou hast blinded mine eyes. How should I know?'

He said to the Linnet, 'Thou canst fly over the tops of the tall trees, and canst see the whole world. Tell me, canst thou see my mother?'

And the Linnet answered, 'Thou hast clipt my wings for thy pleasure. How should I fly?'

And to the little Squirrel who lived in the fir-tree, and was lonely, he said, 'Where is my mother?'

And the Squirrel answered, 'Thou hast slain mine. Dost thou seek to slay thine also?'

And the Star-Child wept and bowed his head, and prayed forgiveness of God's things, and went on through the forest, seeking for the beggar-woman. And on the third day he came to the other side of the forest and went down into the plain.

And when he passed through the villages the children mocked him, and threw stones at him, and the **carlots** would **not suffer him** even to sleep in the **byres** lest he might bring mildew on the stored corn, so foul was he to look at, and their hired men drave him away, and there was none who had pity on him. Nor could he hear anywhere of the beggar-woman who was his mother, though for the space of three years he wandered over the world, and often seemed to see her on the road in front of him, and would call to her, and run after her till the sharp flints made his feet to bleed. But overtake her he could not, and those who **dwelt** by the way did ever deny that they had seen her, or any like to her, and they made sport of his sorrow.

For the space of three years he wandered over the world, and in the world there was neither love nor loving-kindness nor charity for him, but it was even such a world as he had made for himself in the days of his great pride.

And one evening he came to the gate of a strong-walled

city that stood by a river, and, weary and footsore though he was, he made to enter in. But the soldiers who stood on guard dropped their **halberts** across the entrance, and said roughly to him, 'What is thy business in the city?'

'I am seeking for my mother,' he answered, 'and I pray ye to suffer me to pass, for it may be that she is in this city.'

But they mocked at him, and one of them wagged a black beard, and set down his shield and cried, 'Of a truth, thy mother will not be merry when she sees thee, for thou art more ill-favoured than the toad of the marsh, or the adder that crawls in the fen. Get thee gone. Get thee gone. Thy mother dwells not in this city.'

And another, who held a yellow banner in his hand, said to him, 'Who is thy mother, and wherefore art thou seeking for her?'

And he answered, 'My mother is a beggar even as I am, and I have treated her evilly, and I pray ye to suffer me to pass that she may give me her forgiveness, if it be that she **tarrieth** in this city.' But they would not, and pricked him with their spears.

And, as he turned away weeping, one whose armour was inlaid with gilt flowers, and on whose helmet couched a lion that had wings, came up and made inquiry of the soldiers who it was who had sought entrance. And they said to him, 'It is a beggar and the child of a beggar, and we have driven him away.'

'Nay,' he cried, laughing, 'but we will sell the foul thing for a slave, and his price shall be the price of a bowl of sweet wine.'

And an old and evil-visaged man who was passing by called out, and said, 'I will buy him for that price,' and, when he had paid the price, he took the Star-Child by the hand and led him into the city.

And after that they had gone through many streets they came to a little door that was set in a wall that was covered with a pomegranate tree. And the old man touched the door with a ring of graved jasper and it opened, and they went down five steps of brass into a garden filled with black poppies and green jars of burnt clay. And the old man took then from his turban a scarf of figured silk, and bound with it the eyes of the Star-Child, and drave him in front of him. And when the scarf was taken off his eyes, the Star-Child found himself in a dungeon, that was lit by a lantern of horn.

And the old man set before him some mouldy bread on a trencher and said, 'Eat,' and some brackish water in a cup and said, 'Drink,' and when he had eaten and drunk, the old man went out, locking the door behind him and fastening it with an iron chain.

And on the morrow the old man, who was indeed the **subtlest** of the magicians of Libya and had learned his art from one who dwelt in the tombs of the Nile, came in to him and frowned at him, and said, 'In a wood that is nigh to the gate of this city of Giaours there are three pieces of gold. One is of white gold, and another is of yellow gold, and the gold of the third one is red. To-day thou shalt bring me the piece of white gold, and if thou bringest it not back, I will beat thee with a hundred stripes. Get thee away quickly, and at sunset I will be waiting for thee at the door of the garden. See that thou bringest the white gold, or it shall go ill with thee, for thou art my slave, and I have bought thee for the price of a bowl of sweet wine.' And he bound the eyes of the Star-Child with the scarf of figured silk, and led him through the house, and through the garden of poppies, and up the five steps of brass. And having opened the little door with his ring he set him in the street.

And the Star-Child went out of the gate of the city, and came to the wood of which the Magician had spoken to him.

Now this wood was very fair to look at from without, and seemed full of singing birds and of sweet-scented flowers, and the Star-Child entered it gladly. Yet did its beauty profit him little, for wherever he went harsh briars and thorns shot up from the ground and **encompassed** him, and evil nettles stung him, and the thistle pierced him with her daggers, so that he was in sore distress. Nor could he anywhere find the piece of white gold of which the Magician had spoken, though he sought for it from morn to noon, and from noon to sunset. And at sunset he set his face towards home, weeping bitterly, for he knew what fate was in store for him.

But when he had reached the outskirts of the wood, he heard front a thicket a cry as of someone in pain. And forgetting his own sorrow he ran back to the place, and saw there a little Hare caught in a trap that some hunter had set for it.

And the Star-Child had pity on it, and released it, and said to it, 'I am myself but a slave, yet may I give thee thy freedom.'

And the Hare answered him, and said: 'Surely thou hast given me freedom, and what shall I give thee in return?'

And the Star-Child said to it, 'I am seeking for a piece of white gold, nor can I anywhere find it, and if I bring it not to my master he will beat me.'

'Come thou with me,' said the Hare, 'and I will lead thee to it, for I know where it is hidden, and for what purpose.'

So the Star-Child went with the Hare, and lo! in the cleft of a great oak-tree he saw the piece of white gold that he was seeking. And he was filled with joy, and seized it, and said to the Hare, 'The service that I did to thee thou hast **rendered** back again many times over and the kindness that I showed thee thou hast repaid a hundred-fold.'

'Nay,' answered the Hare, 'but as thou dealt with me,

so I did deal with thee,' and it ran away swiftly, and the Star-Child went towards the city.

Now at the gate of the city there was seated one who was a leper. Over his face hung a cowl of grey linen, and through the eyelets his eyes gleamed like red coals. And when he saw the Star-Child coming, he struck upon a wooden bowl, and clattered his bell, and called out to him, and said, 'Give me a piece of money, or I must die of hunger. For they have thrust me out of the city, and there is no one who has pity on me.'

'Alas! cried the Star-Child, 'I have but one piece of money in my wallet, and if I bring it not to my master he will beat me for I am his slave.'

But the leper entreated him, and prayed of him, till the Star-Child had pity, and gave him the piece of white gold.

And when he came to the Magician's house, the Magician opened to him, and brought him in, and said to him, 'Hast thou the piece of white gold?' And the Star-Child answered, 'I have it not.' So the Magician fell upon him, and beat him, and set before him an empty trencher, and said 'Eat,' and an empty cup, and said, 'Drink,' and flung him again into the dungeon.

And on the morrow the Magician came to him, and said, 'If to-day thou bringest me not the piece of yellow gold, I will surely keep thee as my slave, and give thee three hundred stripes.'

So the Star-Child went to the wood, and all day long he searched for the piece of yellow gold, but nowhere could he find it. And at sunset he sat him down and began to weep, and as he was weeping there came to him the little Hare that he had rescued from the trap.

And the Hare said to him, 'Why art thou weeping? And what dost thou seek in the wood?'

And the Star-Child answered, 'I am seeking for a piece of yellow gold that is hidden here, and if I find it not my master will beat me, and keep me as a slave.'

'Follow me,' cried the Hare, and it ran through the wood till it came to a pool of water. And at the bottom of the pool the piece of yellow gold was lying.

'How shall I thank thee?' said the Star-Child, 'for lo! this is the second time that you have **succoured** me.'

'Nay, but thou hadst pity on me first,' said the Hare, and it ran away swiftly.

And the Star-Child took the piece of yellow gold, and put it in his wallet, and hurried to the city. But the leper saw him coming, and ran to meet him and knelt down and cried, 'Give me a piece of money or I shall die of hunger.'

And the Star-Child said to him, 'I have in my wallet but one piece of yellow gold, and if I bring it not to my master he will beat me and keep me as his slave.'

But the leper entreated him sore, so that the Star-Child had pity on him, and gave him the piece of yellow gold.

And when he came to the Magician's house, the Magician opened to him, and brought him in, and said to him, 'Hast thou the piece of yellow gold?' And the Star-Child said to him, 'I have it not.' So the Magician fell upon him, and beat him, and loaded him with chains, and cast him again into the dungeon.

And on the morrow the Magician came to him, and said, 'If to-day thou bringest me the piece of red gold I will set thee free, but if thou bringest it not I will surely slay thee.'

So the Star-Child went to the wood, and all day long he searched for the piece of red gold, but nowhere could he find it. And at evening he sat him down, and wept, and as he was weeping there came to him the little Hare.

And the Hare said to him, 'The piece of red gold that thou seekest is in the cavern that is behind thee. Therefore weep no more but be glad.'

'How shall I reward thee,' cried the Star-Child, 'for lo! this is the third time thou hast succoured me.'

'Nay, but thou hadst pity on me first,' said the Hare, and it ran away swiftly.

And the Star-Child entered the cavern, and in its farthest corner he found the piece of red gold. So he put it in his wallet, and hurried to the city. And the leper seeing him coming, stood in the centre of the road, and cried out, and said to him, 'Give me the piece of red money, or I must die,' and the Star-Child had pity on him again, and gave him the piece of red gold, saying, 'Thy need is greater than mine.' Yet was his heart heavy, for he knew what evil fate awaited him.

But lo! as he passed through the gate of the city, the guards bowed down and made **obeisance** to him, saying, 'How beautiful is our lord!' and a crowd of citizens followed him, and cried out, 'Surely there is none so beautiful in the whole world!' so that the Star-Child wept, and said to himself, 'They are mocking me, and making light of my misery.' And so large was the concourse of the people, that he lost the threads of his way, and found himself at last in a great square, in which there was a palace of a King.

And the gate of the palace opened, and the priests and the high officers of the city ran forth to meet him, and they **abased** themselves before him, and said, 'Thou art our lord for whom we have been waiting, and the son of our King.'

And the Star-Child answered them and said, 'I am no king's son, but the child of a poor beggar-woman. And how say ye that I am beautiful, for I know that I am evil to look at?'

Then he, whose armour was inlaid with gilt flowers, and on whose helmet couched a lion that had wings, held up a shield, and cried, 'How **saith** my lord that he is not beautiful?'

And the Star-Child looked, and lo! his face was even as

it had been, and his comeliness had come back to him, and he saw that in his eyes which he had not seen there before.

And the priests and the high officers knelt down and said to him, 'It was prophesied of old that on this day should come he who was to rule over us. Therefore, let our lord take this crown and this sceptre, and be in his justice and mercy our King over us.'

But he said to them, 'I am not worthy, for I have denied the mother who bare me, nor may I rest till I have found her, and known her forgiveness. Therefore, let me go, for I must wander again over the world, and may not tarry here, though ye bring me the crown and the sceptre.' And as he **spake** he turned his face from them towards the street that led to the gate of the city, and lo! amongst the crowd that pressed round the soldiers, he saw the beggar-woman who was his mother, and at her side stood the leper, who had sat by the road.

And a cry of joy broke from his lips, and he ran over, and kneeling down he kissed the wounds on his mother's feet, and wet them with his tears. He bowed his head in the dust, and sobbing, as one whose heart might break, he said to her: 'Mother, I denied thee in the hour of my pride. Accept me in the hour of my humility. Mother, I gave thee hatred. Do thou give me love. Mother, I rejected thee. Receive thy child now.' But the beggar-woman answered him not a word.

And he reached out his hands, and clasped the white

feet of the leper, and said to him: 'Thrice did I give thee of my mercy. Bid my mother speak to me once.' But the leper answered him not a word.

And he sobbed again, and said: 'Mother, my suffering is greater than I can bear. Give me thy forgiveness, and let me go back to the forest.' And the beggar-woman put her hand on his head, and said to him, 'Rise,' and the leper put his hand on his head, and said to him 'Rise,' also.

And he rose up from his feet, and looked at them, and lo! they were a King and a Queen.

And the Queen said to him, 'This is thy father whom thou hast succoured.'

And the King said, 'This is thy mother, whose feet thou hast washed with thy tears.'

And they fell on his neck and kissed him, and brought him into the palace, and clothed him in fair **raiment**, and set the crown upon his head, and the sceptre in his hand, and over the city that stood by the river he ruled, and was its lord. Much justice and mercy did he show to all, and the evil Magician he banished, and to the Woodcutter and his wife he sent many rich gifts, and to their children he gave high honour. Nor would he suffer any to be cruel to bird or beast, but taught love and loving-kindness and charity, and to the poor he gave bread, and to the naked he gave raiment, and there was peace and plenty in the land.

Yet ruled he not long, so great had been his suffering, and so bitter the fire of his testing, for after the space of three years he died. And he who came after him ruled evilly.

Linnet a type of bird
lustily vigorously
faggots bundles of sticks tied together, used for firewood
deliverance being rescued
aught anything at all
bewailing expressing great sorrow about something
outstripped outpaced
thou art you are
thou hast you have
meet fitting, proper
Godspeed an expression of good wishes to someone undertaking a journey
thee you
alack an expression of dismay
changeling a child who is believed to have been substituted secretly for another, especially by fairies
wroth angry
careth cares
giveth gives
feedeth feeds
cometh comes
morrow the following day
narcissus a type of plant
enamoured fond of
chide to scold someone
dealest deal
wherefore art thou why are you
bade bid
sitteth sits
ill-favoured unattractive or repulsive
cleaving splitting
haggard wood
knowest know
thine yours
sayest say
shalt shall
bare gave birth to
hence from here
beheld saw
drave drove
perchance by some chance
canst can
carlots peasants
not suffer him not allow him
byres barns
dwelt live in a particular place
halberts a weapon combining a spear and a battle-axe
tarrieth tarry, stay in a place for a while longer
subtlest most clever, skilful
encompassed surrounded
rendered given something, especially in return or exchange
succoured given help to in time of need
obeisance a deep bow showing respect
abased humbled
saith say
spake spoke
raiment clothing

The Lizard
by C. J. Cutcliffe Hyne

The Lizard was first published in *The Strand* magazine in 1898. The idea of encounters between people and prehistoric creatures is also explored in Hyne's later novel *The Lost Continent* where the citizens of the lost world of Atlantis have tamed the prehistoric mammoth.

It is not expected that the general public will believe the statements which will be made in this paper. They are written to catch the eye of Mr Wilfred Cecil Cording (or Cordy) if he still lives, or of his friends and relations. Further details may be had from me (by any of these interested people) at Poste Restante, Wharfedale, Yorkshire. My name is Chesney, and I am sufficiently well known there for letters to be forwarded.

The matters in question happened two years ago on the last day of August. I had a small high-ground shoot near Kettlewell, but that morning dense mist made shooting out of the question. However, I wasn't sorry for an off day, as there was a newly-found cave in the neighbourhood which I was anxious to explore — cave hunting being, after shooting, my main amusement.

I suggested to my keeper that he should come with me to inspect the cave: he made some sort of excuse and I did not press the matter further. The dalesman up there look on the local caves with more awe than respect. They will not own up to believing in bogles, but I fancy their creed runs that way. I had taken unwilling helpers cave-hunting with me before, and found them such a nuisance that I didn't press for the keeper's society. So I took candles, matches in a bottle, some **magnesium wire**, a small coil of rope, and a large flask of whisky, and set off alone.

I hadn't seen the cave for a week or more and I was a good deal annoyed to find by the boot marks that quite a lot of people had visited it in the interval. However, I hoped that the larger part of these were made by shepherds, and trusted that I might find the interior still untampered with.

The cave was easy enough to enter. There was a funnel-shaped slide of peat-earth and mud and clay to start with, well pitted with boot marks; and then there was a tumbled wall of boulders, slanting inwards, down which I crawled face uppermost till the light behind me dwindled. The way was getting pretty murky, so I lit up a candle to avoid accidents, stepped knee-deep into a lively stream of water, and went briskly ahead. It was an ordinary enough limestone cave so far, with inferior stalactites, and a good deal of wet everywhere. It did not appear to have been disturbed, and I stepped along cheerfully.

Presently I got a bit of a shock. The roof above began to droop downwards, slowly but relentlessly. It seemed as though my way was soon going to be blocked. However, the water beneath deepened, and so I waded along as far as possible. It was a cold job, the water was up to my chin, and the air was none of the best. I was beginning to think I had got wet through for no adequate result.

But there is no accounting for the freaks of caves. Just when I fancied I was at the end of my tether, I was able to stand erect once more; a dozen yards further on I came out on to dry rock, and was able to have a rest and a drop of whisky. The roof had quite disappeared to candlelight overhead, so I burned a foot of magnesium wire for a better inspection. It was really a magnificent cave.

Well-furnished with stalactites above and stalagmites below: the candle burned brightly, showing me that the air was healthy enough. And yet the air in this cave did not altogether pass muster; there was something new about it, and anything new in cave smells is always suspicious. It wasn't the smell of peat, or iron, or sandstone, or fungus; it was a sort of faint musky smell, rather sickly. When I inhaled a deeper breath of it than usual, it came very near to making my flesh creep.

Before me stretched a tarn of black water, with a beach of white tumbled limestone on the far side.

I pitched a stone into the black water, shattering the surface for the first time during a million years. Yes, it's worth even a year of cave-hunting to do a thing like that.

The stone sank with a luscious *plop*. The water was clearly very deep. But I was wet to the neck already, and didn't mind a swim. So with a lump of clay I stuck one candle in my cap, set up a couple more on the dry rock as a lighthouse to guide my return, lowered myself into the black water, and struck out. The smell of musk oppressed me, and I fancied it was growing stronger. So I didn't dawdle. Roughly, I guessed the pool to be some five-and-thirty yards across.

I landed amongst the broken limestone with a shiver and a scramble: the smell of musk now was strong enough to make me cough. But when I had stood up, got the candle in my hand again, a thrill came through me as I thought I guessed the cause. A dozen yards further on was a broken 'cast,' where some monstrous **uncouth** animal had been entombed in the forgotten ages of the past, and mouldered away and left only the outer shell of its form and shape. For ages this too had endured; indeed it had been violated only by the eroding touch of the water and some earth tremor within the last few days.

A workman with plaster of Paris could make an exact model of this beast which had been lost to the world's knowledge for so many weary millions of years.

It had been some sort of lizard or crocodile, and in

fancy I was beginning to picture its restored shape posed in the National Museum, when my eye fell on something amongst the rubble which brought me to earth with a jar. I stopped and picked it up. It was a common white-handled penknife, of the variety sold by stationers for a shilling. On one side of it was the name of Wilfred Cording (or Cordy), scratched apparently with a nail. The work was neat enough to start with, but the engraver had wearied with his job and the surname was too scratchy to be certain about.

On the hot impulse of the moment, I threw the knife far from me into the black water, and swore. It is more than a little unpleasant for an explorer to find that he has been forestalled. But since then I have more than once regretted the hard things I said against Cording (if that is his name). If the man is alive, I apologise to him. If, as I strongly suspect, he came to a horrible end in the cave, I tender my regrets to his relatives.

I looked upon the cast of the **saurian** now with the warmth of discovery quite gone. I was conscious of cold, and the musky smell was growing more and more unpleasant. I think I should straightway have gone back to daylight and a change of clothes if I hadn't thought I could see the outline of another cast. It was hazy, as a thing of the kind would be if seen through the medium of sparsely transparent limestone, and by the light of a solitary paraffin wax candle. I kicked at it petulantly.

Some flakes of stone shelled off, and I distinctly heard a more extensive crack. I kicked harder – with all my might in fact. More flakes shelled away, and there was a little volley of cracks. It did not feel like kicking against stone. It was like kicking against something that gave. And I could have sworn that the musky smell increased. I felt a curious glow coming over me that was part fright, part excitement, part nausea; but plucked up my courage, and kicked again, and again. The limestone flew up in tinkling showers. There was no doubt now about there being something springy underneath, and that it was the dead carcass of another lizard I hadn't doubt. Here was luck, here was a find. Here was I the discoverer of the body of a prehistoric beast, preserved in the limestone down through all the ages just as mammoths have been preserved in Siberian ice.

As I kicked and battered at the harsh, scaly skin of this **anachronism**, which ought to have perished body and bones ten million years ago, I remember wondering whether they would make me a baronet for the discovery.

Then of a sudden I got a **start**. I could have sworn the dead flesh moved beneath me.

But I shouted aloud at myself in contempt.

Ten million years: it was impossible. And then I got a further start, a more solid one. While I was raising a boulder for a further blow, a splinter of stone broke away as if pressed up from below, flipped up in the air. My blood chilled, and for a moment the loneliness of that unknown cave oppressed me. But I told myself that I was an old hand; that this was childishness. I continued my battering until a further movement left me in no possible doubt – the beast was actually stirring of its own accord.

Stirring – and alive. It was writhing, and straining to leave its rocky bed where it had lain quiet through all those countless cycles of time, and I watched it in a very **petrifaction** of terror. Its efforts threw up whole baskets full of splintered stone at a time. I could see the muscles of its back ripple at each effort. I could see the exposed part of its body grow in size every time it wrenched at the walls of that semi-eternal prison.

Then, as I looked, it doubled up its back like a bucking horse, and drew out its stumpy head and long feelers, giving out the while a thin, small scream like a hurt child; and then with another effort it pulled out its long tail and stood upon the debris of the limestone, panting with a new-found life.

I gazed upon it with a sickly fascination. Its body was about the bigness of two horses. Its head was curiously short, but the mouth opened back almost to the forearm; and sprouting from the nose were two enormous feelers, each at least 6 ft. long, tipped with fleshy tendrils like fingers, which opened and shut tremulously. In colour it was a bright grass-green. And worst of all was the musky smell. All this while I had stood motionless but the beast must have heard some slight movement. I could not see any ears, but it heard me, no doubt of that. Worse, it hobbled round clumsily with its jointless legs, and waved its feelers in my direction. I could not make out any eyes; its sensitiveness seemed to lie in those fathom-long feelers and in the fleshy fingers which twitched at the end of them.

Then it opened its great jaws and yawned cavernously, and came towards me. It seemed to have no trace of fear or hesitation. It hobbled clumsily on, exhibiting its monstrous deformity in every movement, and preceded always by those hateful feelers.

For a while I stayed in my place, too paralysed with horror at this awful thing I had dragged up from the forgotten dead. But then one of its feelers touched me, and the fleshy fingers pawed my face. I leaped into movement again. The beast was hungry after its fast of ten million years . . . I turned and ran.

It followed me. In the feeble light of the one solitary candle I could see it hobbling – and hobbling faster and less clumsily now as it worked the rust of ages out of its **cankered** joints. Presently it was following me with a speed equal to my own.

If this huge beast had shown anger, eagerness, any feelings, it would have been less horrible; but it was absolutely unemotional in its hunt, and this in turn came near to making me feel that I was lost, that I should surrender myself to the inevitable. I wondered dully whether there had been another beast entombed beside it, and whether that had eaten the man who owned the penknife.

But the thought suggested an idea to me. I had a stout knife in my own pocket, and I drew it out and turned to defend myself just as the feelers with their fringe of fumbling fingers were agonisingly close to me. I slashed at them viciously, and felt my knife grate against their armour. I might as well have hacked at an iron rail.

Still the attempt did me good. There is an animal love of fighting stowed away in the bottom of all of us somewhere, and mine woke then. I don't know that I expected to win; but I did intend to do the largest possible amount of damage before I was caught. I made a rush, stepped with one foot on the beast's creeping back, and leaped astern of him: the beast gave its thin, small whistling scream, and turned quickly in chase.

We doubled, turned, sprawled, leapt among the slimy boulders, and every time we came to close quarters I stabbed with my knife, without ever finding a joint in its armour.

It was clear that this could not go on. The beast grew in strength and activity, and probably in dumb anger, though it gave no sign of it; but I meanwhile was growing more blown, more bruised, more exhausted every moment.

At last I tripped and fell. The beast with its clumsy waddle shot past me before it could pull up, and in desperation I threw one arm up to drive the knife with the full of my force into the underneath part of its body.

That woke it at last. It writhed, and it plunged, and it bucked with a frenzy that I had never seen before, and its scream grew in piercingness till it was strong as the whistle of a steam engine. Again and again I planted my vicious blows until it shook itself free in desperation and set off at its hobbling gait directly for the water.

It plunged in, swam briskly with its tail, then I saw it dive and disappear for good.

And what next? I took to the water too, and swam as I had never swam before. It was that or nothing – risk the swim, or stay and be eaten. How I got across I do not know. How I landed I do not know. How I got down the windings of the cave is more than I can say and whether the beast followed me I do not know either. Somehow I got to daylight again, staggering like a drunken man. I struggled as far as the village, noting how the people ran from me. At the inn the landlord cried out as though I had been the plague. It seemed that the musky smell that I brought with me was unendurable, though by this time the mere detail of a smell was far beneath my notice. But I was stripped from my stinking clothes and washed and put to bed, and a doctor came and gave me an opiate; and when twelve hours later wakefulness came to me again,

I had the sense to hold my tongue. All the village wanted to know where the smell came from. I said 'I must have fallen into something.'

And there the matter ends for the moment. I go no more cave-hunting, and I offer no help to those who do. But if the man who owned that white-handled penknife is alive, I should like to compare experiences with him.

---

bogles ghosts
creed beliefs
magnesium wire a thin ribbon of metal used in lamps as a source of light
qualms misgivings, worries
emulation trying to do something as well as others, especially by copying them
tarn a small mountain lake
vignetted faded away
uncouth rough in manner
saurian animal resembling a lizard
anachronism something wrongly placed in a particular historical period
start shock
petrifaction being turned into a fossil
callosities areas of thickened skin
endued endowed
gait way of walking
cankered diseased or bad-tempered

Realist stories

The 19th century was a time of great change. The urban population grew rapidly as people moved to towns and cities in search of work and the rural landscape was transformed by the introduction of the railway and new farming methods and machinery. This social upheaval transformed people's lives and the new realities they faced were reflected in the fiction of the time.

London loomed large in many novels and short stories, with Charles Dickens chronicling the lives of rich and poor alike amidst the capital's streets in his celebrated works *Oliver Twist*, *Bleak House* and *Great Expectations* to name but a few. The term 'Dickensian' was coined to describe the poverty-stricken lives he depicted, with other writers exploring these social conditions in their fiction.

Like Charles Dickens, Arthur Morrison was a journalist and author of fiction who explored the reality of working-class life in London's East End in the late 19th century. In his short story included in this collection, 'Behind the Shade', Morrison depicts the fine line that exists between a seemingly respectable life and the grim consequences of poverty.

The changes that transformed rural life were also

reflected in 19th-century fiction. In Emily Brontë's novel *Wuthering Heights* the wildness of the Yorkshire moors provides a backdrop for a stormy romance, whilst Elizabeth Gaskell's *North and South* contrasts country life and the lives of city-dwellers.

Thomas Hardy was a writer who explored the harsh realities of rural life in his novels and short stories. From the plight of farm workers to the way Victorian society treated women, his stories explore and criticize the beliefs and attitudes of the time. In his story, 'The Tradition of Eighteen Hundred and Four', his narrator looks back to the beginning of the 19th century to describe a secret visit to England made by the French military leader Napoleon Bonaparte, to plan an invasion of the country.

Behind the Shade
by Arthur Morrison

Behind the Shade was first published in 1893 in the
National Observer, a 19th-century newspaper. The story
was later collected in *Tales of Mean Streets*, a collection
of Arthur Morrison's short stories about East End life.
As a journalist, Morrison drew on his keen powers
of observation to depict the harsh realities of life for
working-class people.

The street was the common East End street — two parallels
of brick pierced with windows and doors. But at the end
of one, where the builder had found a remnant of land
too small for another six-roomer, there stood an odd box
of a cottage, with three rooms and a wash-house. It had a
green door with a well-blacked knocker round the corner;
and in the lower window in front stood a 'shade of fruit'—
a cone of waxen grapes and apples under a glass cover.

Although the house was smaller than the others, and
was built upon a remnant, it was always a house of some
consideration. In a street like this mere independence of
pattern gives distinction. And a house inhabited by one
sole family makes a figure among houses inhabited by
two or more, even though it be the smallest of all. And

here the seal of respectability was set by the shade of fruit — a sign accepted in those parts. Now, when people keep a house to themselves, and keep it clean; when they neither stand at the doors nor gossip across back-fences; when, moreover, they have a well-dusted shade of fruit in the front window; and, especially, when they are two women who tell nobody their business: they are known at once for well-to-do, and are regarded with the **admixture** of spite and respect that is proper to the circumstances. They are also watched.

Still, the neighbours knew the history of the Perkinses, mother and daughter, in its main features, with little disagreement: having told it to each another, filling in the details when occasion seemed to serve. Perkins, ere he died, had been a **shipwright**; and this was when shipwrights were the aristocracy of the work-shops, and he that worked more than three or four days a week was counted a mean slave; it was long (in fact) before depression, strikes, iron plates, and collective blindness had driven shipbuilding to the Clyde. Perkins had laboured no harder than his fellows, had married a tradesman's daughter, and had spent his money with freedom; and some while after his death his widow and daughter came to live in the small house, and kept a school for tradesmen's little girls in a back room over the wash-house. But as the School Board **waxed** in power, and the tradesmen's pride in regard **thereunto waned**, the attendance, never large, came down to twos and threes. Then Mrs Perkins met with her accident. A dweller in Stidder's Rents overtook her one night, and, having vigorously punched her in the face and the breast, kicked her and jumped on her for five minutes as she lay on the pavement. (In the dark, it afterwards appeared, he had mistaken her for his mother.) The one distinct opinion the adventure bred in the street was Mrs Webster's, the Little **Bethelite**, who considered it a judgment for sinful pride — for Mrs Perkins had been a churchgoer. But the neighbours never saw Mrs Perkins again. The doctor left his patient "as well as she ever would be," but bed-ridden and helpless. Her daughter was a scraggy, sharp-faced woman of thirty or so, whose black dress hung from her hips as from a wooden frame; and some people got into the way of calling her Mrs Perkins, seeing no other thus to honour. And, meantime, the school had ceased, although Miss Perkins **essayed** a revival, and joined a **Dissenting chapel** to that end.

Then, one day, a card appeared in the window, over the shade of fruit, with the legend 'Pianoforte Lessons'. It was not approved by the street. It was a standing advertisement of the fact that the Perkinses had a piano, which others had not. It also revealed a **grasping** spirit on the part of people able to keep a house to themselves, with red curtains and a shade of fruit in the parlour window; who, moreover, had been able to give up keeping a school because of ill-health. The pianoforte lessons were **eight-and-sixpence** a quarter, two a week. Nobody was ever known to take them but the relieving officer's daughter, and she paid sixpence a lesson, to see how she got on, and left off in three weeks. The card stayed in the window a fortnight longer, and none of the neighbours saw the cart that came in the night and took away the old cabinet piano with the channelled keys, that had been fourth-hand when Perkins bought it twenty years ago. Mrs Clark, the widow who sewed far into the night, may possibly have heard a noise and looked; but she said nothing if she did. There was no card in the window next morning, but the shade of fruit stood primly respectable as ever. The curtains were drawn a little closer across, for some of the children playing in the street were used to flatten their faces against the lower panes, and to discuss the piano, the stuff-bottomed chairs, the **antimacassars**, the mantelpiece ornaments, and the loo table with the family Bible and the album on it.

It was soon after this that the Perkinses altogether ceased from shopping — ceased, at any rate, in that neighbourhood. Trade with them had already been dwindling, and it was said that Miss Perkins was getting stingier than her mother — who had been stingy enough herself. Indeed, the Perkins demeanour began to change for the worse, to be significant of a miserly retirement and an offensive alienation from the rest of the street.

One day the deacon called, as was his practice now and then; but, being invited no further than the doorstep, he went away in **dudgeon**, and did not return. Nor, indeed, was Miss Perkins seen again at chapel.

Then there was a discovery. The **spare** figure of Miss Perkins was seldom seen in the streets, and then almost always at night; but on these occasions she was observed to carry parcels of varying wrappings and shapes. Once, in broad daylight, with a package in newspaper, she made such haste past a shop-window where stood Mrs Webster and Mrs Jones, that she tripped on the broken sole of one shoe, and fell headlong. The newspaper broke away from its pins, and although the woman reached and recovered her parcel before she rose, it was plain to see that it was made up of cheap shirts, cut out ready for the stitching. The street had the news the same hour, and it was generally held that such a taking of the bread out of the mouths of them that wanted it by them that had plenty was a scandal and a shame, and ought to be put a stop to. And Mrs Webster, foremost in the setting right of things, undertook to find out whence the work came, and to say a few plain words in the right **quarter**.

All this while nobody watched closely enough to note that the parcels brought in were fewer than the parcels taken out. Even a hand-truck, late one evening, went unremarked: the door being round the corner, and most people within. One morning, though, Miss Perkins, her best foot foremost, was venturing along a near street with an outgoing parcel — large and triangular and wrapped in white **drugget** — when the **relieving officer** turned the corner across the way.

The relieving officer was a man in whose system of etiquette the Perkinses had caused some little disturbance. His ordinary female acquaintances (not, of course, professional) he was in the habit of recognizing by a gracious nod. When he met the minister's wife he lifted his hat, instantly assuming an intense frown, in the event of **irreverent observation**. Now he quite felt that the Perkinses were entitled to some advance upon the nod, although it would be absurd to raise them to a level with the minister's wife. So he had long since established a compromise: he closed his finger and thumb upon the brim of his hat, and let his hand fall forthwith. Preparing now to accomplish this salute, he was astounded to see that Miss Perkins, as soon as she was aware of his approach, turned her face, which was rather flushed, away from him, and went hurrying onward, looking at the wall on her side of the street. The relieving officer, checking his hand on its way to his hat, stopped and looked after her as she turned the corner, hugging her parcel on the side next the wall. Then he shouldered his umbrella and pursued his way, holding his head high, and staring fiercely straight before him; for a relieving officer is not used to being **cut**.

It was a little after this that Mr Crouch, the landlord, called. He had not been calling regularly, because of late Miss Perkins had left her five shillings of rent with Mrs Crouch every Saturday evening. He noted with satisfaction the whitened sills and the shade of fruit, behind which the curtains were now drawn close and pinned together. He turned the corner and lifted the bright knocker. Miss Perkins half opened the door, stood in the opening, and began to speak.

His jaw dropped. "Beg pardon — forgot something. Won't wait — call next week — do just as well." And he hurried round the corner and down the street, puffing and blowing and staring. "Why, the woman frightened me," he afterward explained to Mrs Crouch. "There's something wrong with her eyes, and she looked like a corpse. The rent wasn't ready — I could see that before she spoke; so I cleared out."

"P'r'aps something's happened to the old lady," suggested Mrs Crouch. "Anyhow, I should thing the rent 'ud be all right." And he thought it would.

Nobody saw the Perkinses that week. The shade of fruit stood in its old place, but was thought not to have been dusted after Tuesday. Certainly the sills and the doorstep were neglected. Friday, Saturday and Sunday were swallowed up in a choking brown fog, wherein men lost their bearings, and fell into docks, and stepped over embankment edges. It was as though a great blot had fallen, and had obliterated three days from the calendar. It cleared on Monday morning, and, just as the women in the street were sweeping their steps, Mr Crouch was seen at the green door. He lifted the knocker, dull and sticky now with the foul vapour, and knocked a gentle rat-tat. There was no answer. He knocked again, a little louder, and waited, listening. But there was neither voice nor movement within. He gave three heavy knocks, and then came round to the front window. There was the shade of fruit, the glass a little duller on the top, the curtains pinned close about it, and nothing to see beyond them. He tapped at the window with his knuckles, and backed into the roadway to look at the one above. This was a window with a striped holland blind and a short net curtain; but never a face was there.

The sweepers stopped to look, and one from opposite came and reported that she had seen nothing of Miss Perkins for a week, and that certainly nobody had left the house that morning. And Mr Crouch grew excited, and bellowed through the keyhole.

In the end they opened the sash-fastening with a knife, moved the shade of fruit, and got in. The room was bare and empty, and their steps and voices resounded as those of people in an unfurnished house. The wash-house was vacant, but it was clean, and there was a little net curtain in the window. The short passage and the stairs were bare boards. In the back room by the stair-head was a drawn window-blind, and that was all. In the front room, with the striped blind and the short curtain, there was a bed of rags and old newspapers; also a wooden box; and on each of these was a dead woman.

Both deaths, the doctor found, were from **syncope**, the result of **inanition**; and the better-nourished woman — she on the bed — had died the sooner; perhaps by a day or two. The other case was rather curious; it exhibited a degree of shrinkage in the digestive organs unprecedented in his experience. After the inquest the street had an evening's fame; for the papers printed coarse drawings of the house, and in **leaderettes** demanded the abolition of something. Then it became its wonted self. And it was doubted if the waxen apples and the curtains fetched enough to pay Mr Crouch his fortnight's rent.

---

admixture state of being mixed
shipwright shipbuilder
waxed increased
thereunto to that place
waned weakened
Bethelite Jehovah's Witness
essayed attempted
Dissenting chapel a non-conformist church
grasping greedy for money
eight-and-sixpence eight shillings and six pence (worth approximately £50 today)
antimacassars pieces of cloth placed over the back and arms of chairs to protect them from wear

dudgeon resentment or indignation
spare thin
quarter an unspecified person or group of people
drugget a coarse woolen fabric used as a floor covering
relieving officer an official appointed by a parish to give aid to the poor
irreverent observation a comment lacking respect
cut ignored
syncope loss of consciousness caused by a fall in blood pressure
inanition exhaustion caused by lack of nourishment
leaderettes editorials

A Tradition of Eighteen Hundred and Four by **Thomas Hardy**

First published in 1882, *A Tradition of Eighteen Hundred and Four* looks back to the beginning of the 19th-century and a time when Britain was at war with France. Although the story describes an imagined visit by the French military leader Napoleon Bonaparte, Hardy's tale reflects concerns about invasion that were commonplace in the last decades of the 19th century and the first decade of the 20th, leading up to the outbreak of the First World War in 1914.

The widely discussed possibility of an invasion of England through a Channel tunnel has more than once recalled old Solomon Selby's story to my mind.

The occasion on which I numbered myself among his audience was one evening when he was sitting in the yawning chimney-corner of the inn-kitchen, with some others who had gathered there, and I entered for shelter from the rain. Withdrawing the stem of his pipe from the dental notch in which it habitually rested, he leaned back in the recess behind him and smiled into the fire. The smile was neither mirthful nor sad, not precisely humourous nor altogether thoughtful. We who knew him recognized it in a moment: it was his narrative smile. Breaking off our few **desultory** remarks we drew up closer, and he thus began:—

"My father, as you mid know, was a shepherd all his life, and lived out by the Cove four miles yonder, where I was born and lived likewise, till I moved here shortly **afore** I was married. The cottage that first knew me stood on the top of the down, near the sea; there was no house within a mile and a half of it; it was built o' purpose for the farm-shepherd, and had no other use. They tell me that it is now pulled down, but that you can see where it stood by the mounds of earth and a few broken bricks that are still lying about. It was a bleak and dreary place in winter-time, but in summer it was well enough, though the garden never came to much, because we could not get up a good shelter for the vegetables and currant bushes; and where there is much wind they don't thrive.

"Of all the years of my growing up the ones that **bide** clearest in my mind were eighteen hundred and three, four, and five. This was for two reasons: I had just then grown to an age when a child's eyes and ears take in and note down everything about him, and there was more at that date to bear in mind than there ever has been since with me. It was, as I need hardly tell ye, the time after the first peace, when **Bonaparte** was scheming his descent upon England. He had crossed the great Alp mountains, fought in Egypt, **drubbed** the Turks, the Austrians, and the **Proossians**, and now thought he'd have a slap at us. On the other side of the Channel, scarce out of sight and hail of a man standing on our English shore, the French army of a hundred and sixty thousand men and fifteen thousand horses had been brought together from all parts, and were drilling every day. Bonaparte had been three years a-making his preparations; and to ferry these soldiers and cannon and horses across he had contrived a couple of thousand flat-bottomed boats. These boats were small things, but wonderfully built. A good few of 'em were so made as to have a little stable on board each for the two horses that were to haul the cannon carried at the stern. To get in order all these, and other things required, he had assembled there five or six thousand fellows that worked at trades--carpenters, blacksmiths, wheelwrights, saddlers, and what not. O 'twas a curious time!

"Every morning Neighbour **Boney** would muster his multitude of soldiers on the beach, draw 'em up in line, practise 'em in the manoeuvre of embarking, horses and all, till they could do it without a single hitch. My father drove a flock of ewes up into Sussex that year, and as he went along the **drover's track** over the high downs thereabout he could see this drilling actually going on — the **accoutrements** of the rank and file glittering in the sun like silver. It was thought and always said by my uncle Job, sergeant of foot (who used to know all about these matters), that Bonaparte meant to cross with oars on a calm night. The grand query with us was, Where would my gentleman land? Many of the common people thought it would be at Dover; others, who knew how unlikely it was that any skilful general would make a business of landing just where he was expected, said he'd go either east into the River Thames, or west'ard to some convenient place, most likely one of the little bays inside the Isle of Portland, between the Beal and St. Alban's Head — and for choice the three-quarter-round Cove, screened from every mortal eye, that seemed made o' purpose, out by where we lived, and which I've **climmed** up with two tubs of brandy across my shoulders on scores o' dark nights in my younger days. Some had heard that a part o' the French fleet would sail right round Scotland, and come up the Channel to a suitable haven. However, there was much doubt upon the matter; and no wonder, for after-years proved that Bonaparte himself could hardly make up his mind upon that great and very particular point, where to land. His uncertainty came about in this wise, that he could get no news as to where and how our troops lay in waiting, and that his knowledge of possible places where flat-bottomed boats might be quietly run ashore, and the men they brought marshalled in order, was dim to the last degree. Being flat-bottomed, they didn't require a harbour for unshipping their cargo of men, but a good shelving beach away from sight, and with a fair open road toward London. How the question posed that great **Corsican tyrant** (as we used to call him), what pains he took to settle it, and, above all, what a risk he ran on one particular night in trying to do so, were known only to one man here and there; and certainly to no maker of newspapers or printer of books, or my account o't would not have had so many heads shaken over it as it has by **gentry** who only believe what they see in printed lines.

"The flocks my father had charge of fed all about the downs near our house, overlooking the sea and shore each way for miles. In winter and early spring father was up a deal at nights, watching and tending the lambing. Often he'd go to bed early, and turn out at twelve or one; and on the other hand, he'd sometimes stay up till twelve or one, and then turn in to bed. As soon as I was old enough I used to help him, mostly in the way of keeping an eye upon the ewes while he was gone home to rest. This is what I was doing in a particular month in either the year four or five — I can't certainly fix which, but it was long before I was took away from the sheepkeeping to be bound prentice to a trade. Every night at that time I was at the fold, about half a mile, or it may be a little more, from our cottage, and no living thing at all with me but the ewes and young lambs. **Afeard**? No; I was never afeard of being alone at these times; for I had been reared in such an out-step place that the lack o' human beings at night made me less fearful than the sight of 'em. Directly I saw a man's shape after dark in a lonely place I was frightened out of my senses.

"One day in that month we were surprised by a visit from my uncle Job, the sergeant in the **Sixty-first foot**, then in camp on the downs above **King George's watering-place**, several miles to the west yonder. Uncle Job dropped in about dusk, and went up with my father to the fold for an hour or two. Then he came home, had a drop to drink from the tub of **sperrits** that the smugglers kept us in for housing their liquor when they'd made a run, and for burning 'em off when there was danger. After that he stretched himself out on the settle to sleep. I went to bed: at one o'clock father came home, and waking me to go and take his place, according to custom, went to bed himself. On my way out of the house I passed Uncle Job on the settle. He opened his eyes, and upon my telling him where I was going he said it was a shame that such a youngster as I should go up there all alone; and when he had fastened up his stock and waist-belt he set off along with me, taking a drop from the sperrit-tub in a little flat bottle that stood in the corner-cupboard.

"By and by we drew up to the **fold**, saw that all was

right, and then, to keep ourselves warm, curled up in a heap of straw that lay inside the thatched hurdles we had set up to break the stroke of the wind when there was any. To-night, however, there was none. It was one of those very still nights when, if you stand on the high hills anywhere within two or three miles of the sea, you can hear the rise and fall of the tide along the shore, coming and going every few moments like a sort of great snore of the sleeping world. Over the lower ground there was a bit of a mist, but on the hill where we lay the air was clear, and the moon, then in her last quarter, flung a fairly good light on the grass and scattered straw.

"While we lay there Uncle Job amused me by telling me strange stories of the wars he had served in and the **wownds** he had got. He had already fought the French in the **Low Countries**, and hoped to fight 'em again. His stories lasted so long that at last I was hardly sure that I was not a soldier myself, and had seen such service as he told of. The wonders of his tales quite bewildered my mind, till I fell asleep and dreamed of battle, smoke, and flying soldiers, all of a kind with the doings he had been bringing up to me.

"How long my nap lasted I am not prepared to say. But some faint sounds over and above the rustle of the ewes in the straw, the bleat of the lambs, and the tinkle of the sheep-bell brought me to my waking senses. Uncle

Job was still beside me; but he too had fallen asleep. I looked out from the straw, and saw what it was that had aroused me. Two men, in boat-cloaks, cocked hats, and swords, stood by the hurdles about twenty yards off.

"I turned my ear **thitherward** to catch what they were saying, but though I heard every word o't, not one did I understand. They spoke in a tongue that was not ours — in French, as I afterward found. But if I could not gain the meaning of a word, I was shrewd boy enough to find out a deal of the talkers' business. By the light o' the moon I could see that one of 'em carried a roll of paper in his hand, while every moment he spoke quick to his comrade, and pointed right and left with the other hand to spots along the shore. There was no doubt that he was explaining to the second gentleman the shapes and features of the coast. What happened soon after made this still clearer to me.

"All this time I had not waked Uncle Job, but now I began to be afeared that they might **light upon** us, because uncle breathed so heavily **through's** nose. I put my mouth to his ear and whispered, 'Uncle Job.'

"'What is it, my boy?' he said, just as if he hadn't been asleep at all.

"'Hush!' says I. 'Two French generals —'

"'French?' says he.

"'Yes,' says I. 'Come to see where to land their army!'

"I pointed 'em out; but I could say no more, for the

pair were coming at that moment much nearer to where we lay. As soon as they got as near as eight or ten yards, the officer with a roll in his hand stooped down to a slanting hurdle, unfastened his roll upon it, and spread it out. Then suddenly he sprung a dark lantern open on the paper, and showed it to be a map.

"'What be they looking at?' I whispered to Uncle Job.

"'A chart of the Channel,' says the sergeant (knowing about such things).

"The other French officer now stooped likewise, and over the map they had a long consultation, as they pointed here and there on the paper, and then hither and thither at places along the shore beneath us. I noticed that the manner of one officer was very respectful toward the other, who seemed much his superior, the second in rank calling him by a sort of title that I did not know the sense of. The head one, on the other hand, was quite familiar with his friend, and more than once clapped him on the shoulder.

"Uncle Job had watched as well as I, but though the map had been in the lantern-light, their faces had always been in shade. But when they rose from stooping over the chart the light flashed upward, and fell smart upon one of 'em's features. No sooner had this happened than Uncle Job gasped, and sank down as if he'd been in a fit.

"'What is it — what is it, Uncle Job?' said I.

"'O good God!' says he, under the straw.

"'What?' says I.

"'Boney!' he groaned out.

"'Who?' says I.

"'Bonaparty,' he said. 'The Corsican ogre. O that I had got but my new-flinted **firelock**, that there man should die! But I haven't got my new-flinted firelock, and that there man must live. So lie low, as you value your life!'

"I did lie low, as you mid suppose. But I couldn't help peeping. And then I too, lad as I was, knew that it was the face of Bonaparte. Not know Boney? I should think I did know Boney. I should have known him by half the light o' that lantern. If I had seen a picture of his features once, I had seen it a hundred times. There was his bullet head, his short neck, his round yaller cheeks and chin, his gloomy face, and his great glowing eyes. His took off his hat to blow himself a bit, and there was the forelock in the middle of his forehead, as in all the **draughts** of him. In moving, his cloak fell a little open, and I could see for a moment his white-fronted jacket and one of his **epaulets**.

"But none of this lasted long. In a minute he and his general had rolled up the map, shut the lantern, and turned to go down toward the shore.

"Then Uncle Job came to himself a bit. 'Slipped across in the night-time to see how to put his men ashore,' he said. 'The like o' that man's coolness eyes will never again see! Nephew, I must act in this, and immediate, or England's lost!'

"When they were over the brow, we **crope** out, and went some little way to look after them. Halfway down they were joined by two others, and six or seven minutes brought them to the shore. Then, from behind a rock, a boat came out into the weak moonlight of the Cove, and they jumped in; it put off instantly, and vanished in a few minutes between the two rocks that stand at the mouth of the Cove as we all know. We climmed back to where we had been before, and I could see, a little way out, a larger vessel, though still not very large. The little boat drew up alongside, was made fast at the stern as I suppose, for the largest sailed away, and we saw no more.

"My uncle Job told his officers as soon as he got back to camp; but what they thought of it I never heard — neither did he. Boney's army never came, and a good job for me; for the Cove below my father's house was where he meant to land, as this secret visit showed. We coast-folk should have been cut down one and all, and I should not have sat here to tell this tale."

We who listened to old Selby that night have been familiar with his simple grave-stone for these ten years past. Thanks to the **incredulity** of the age his tale has been seldom repeated. But if anything short of the direct testimony of his own eyes could persuade an **auditor** that Bonaparte had examined these shores for himself

221

with a view to a practicable landing-place, it would have been Solomon Selby's manner of narrating the adventure which **befell** him on the down.

Christmas 1882.

---

desultory half-hearted, without enthusiasm or a definite plan
afore before
bide stay
Bonaparte Napoleon Bonaparte, the French Emperor between 1804 and 1815
drubbed beat, defeated
Proossians Prussians, citizens of Prussia (now part of modern Germany)
Boney slang term used by the British to refer to Napoleon Bonaparte
drover's track route for transporting livestock
accoutrements military equipment
climmed climbed
Corsican tyrant cruel ruler (Napoleon was from the island of Corsica)
gentry people of a good social position
afeard afraid
Sixty-first foot an infantry regiment in the British army
King George's watering-place a reference to the town of Weymouth where King George spent his summer holidays
sperrits spirits, alcohol
fold an enclosure for sheep
wownds wounds
Low Countries the name for the region of Europe comprising the Netherlands, Belgium and Luxembourg
thitherward towards that place
light upon discover
through's through his
firelock firearm, weapon
draughts drawings, pictures
epaulets ornamental shoulder decorations worn on military uniforms
crope crept
incredulity the state of being unable to believe something is true
auditor listener
befell happened to